EXIT MURDERER

EXIT MURDERER

Sara Woods

Exit Murderer
(stage direction)
Macbeth, Act III, scene iv

St. Martin's Press
New York

Any work of fiction whose characters were of uniform excellence
would rightly be condemned—by that fact if by no other—as being
incredibly dull. Therefore no excuse can be considered necessary for
the villainy or folly of the people appearing in this book. It seems
extremely unlikely that any one of them should resemble a real
person, alive or dead. Any such resemblance is completely
unintentional and without malice.

S.W.

Library of Congress Catalog Card Number 77-17767

ISBN 0-312-27588-9

Author's Note

Once upon a time Mr. Antony Maitland, of Counsel, encountered, briefly and dangerously, in the preparation of one of his cases, a man then unknown to him except as the leader of an organisation which devoted itself, with great profit, to the smuggling of diamonds. This is the story of what happened six years later, when he met that man again.

S.W.

THURSDAY, 20th MAY

I

'You see, I more or less gave my word to Sykes that I'd take the case,' said Antony Maitland. He succeeded in sounding at once both stubborn and apologetic. His uncle, Sir Nicholas Harding, ignoring the note of apology, went straight to what seemed to him to be the heart of the matter.

'You don't like the West Midland circuit, you're not popular in Chedcombe – '

'It's not Chedcombe, it's Northdean.'

' – and you are under no obligation to do favours for the police,' concluded Sir Nicholas, ignoring the interruption.

'Sykes has always been helpful,' Maitland pointed out.

'Which is no doubt why the Chief Inspector was chosen to put the matter before you. But the case does not directly concern him – '

'Except in so far as the good name of the police force in general concerns him.'

' – and you've never heard of this Inspector Brady, as far as I know.'

'You're right about that, of course. He's the local Divisional Detective Inspector, but the only member of the Northdean police I've ever had dealings with is in the uniform branch . . . a chap called Mawson, as far as I remember.'

'That is all beside the point,' said Sir Nicholas with some acerbity. 'If you can give me one good reason – '

'I can give you three.' He paused, hopefully, but his uncle only waited in silence and after a moment he went on. 'I've dealt with a wrongful arrest case before on behalf of the police; I know the local solicitor, Peter Gibson, who is apparently anxious to brief me, though I can't quite see why; and

7

the case you dealt with six years ago in Northdean, when I was devilling for you, concerned diamond smuggling, which is exactly what seems to have erupted again.'

'That is the very reason why . . . but you'd better tell me about it.' Sir Nicholas sounded resigned, but his nephew knew him too well to be deceived by that.

'I don't know too much about it myself,' he said, concealing well enough his dislike of being forced into a position where explanations were inevitable. 'If you ask me, I think Sykes was being deliberately vague. A chap called Dobell was accused of diamond smuggling – I told you that – with a John Irving as co-defendant. The investigating officer, the chief prosecution witness at the trial, was this Inspector Brady; unfortunately, none of the supporting witnesses came up to proof, both of the accused were acquitted, and after apparently thinking things over for a week or two they decided to bring a charge of wrongful arrest.'

'It seems a little odd . . . as I remember it, Chief Inspector Sykes was very anxious on that previous occasion, when we were together in Northdean, to dissuade you from taking any part in the investigation.'

'Well – ' said Antony, and left it there. His uncle smiled at him. If a third party had been present he might have seen at that moment the resemblance very strong between them; and very likely been puzzled by it, as it was one of expression only. Both were tall men, but apart from that there was no physical resemblance between them. Maitland was dark, with a casual air and a humorous look that perhaps at the moment was a little overlaid by anxiety; his uncle was more heavily built, and his hair was so fair that what grey there was in it did not show at all. He had, besides, an air of authority about him, of which he was completely unconscious.

'Precisely,' he said now, just as though his nephew had actually completed the sentence. 'He thought it was too dangerous.'

'He doesn't think that this time. There's no question of

my investigations going further than the circumstances or the charge, and the acquittal.'

'Knowing you – as I thought Sykes did – ' Sir Nicholas too failed to complete his thought. 'He, of course, knew nothing of the lunatic impulse that brought you into contact with the man whose name we never knew, but who was clearly the master-mind – if I may borrow an expression from fiction – behind the whole illicit trade in diamonds.'

'You may as well call him Mr. X and be done with it,' Antony advised him. 'Of course I didn't tell Sykes about that. If you remember I made a deal with him, something I'm sure the police would have frowned on.'

'All the same, he was a dangerous man, you admitted as much to me at the time. To embroil yourself deliberately in his affairs – '

'We've no reason to think he's concerned in any way.'

'Don't be disingenuous, Antony. If you think about it we have every reason. One outlet in Northdean was closed to him, he found another. It's as simple as that.'

'Perhaps it is, but there's no earthly reason why our paths should cross again.'

'He knows you, remember; you don't know him.'

'Well, come to that, I'm more likely to bump into him in the street here in London than I am in Northdean. That could happen at any time, and would prove embarrassing to both of us.'

'I can see,' said Sir Nicholas, declining to have anything to do with this piece of special pleading, 'that your mind is made up.'

'I told you, I promised Sykes.'

'Then I shall say no more about it.' Antony grinned at that, he didn't believe it for a moment. 'Who is the local solicitor? You said you know him.'

'Peter Gibson. He was Camilla Barnard's solicitor, you must remember him yourself. It was his brother-in-law you finally exposed in court.'

'Of course I remember.' Sir Nicholas, however, seemed

9

to find no pleasure in the recollection. 'The whole preparation of the case was grossly mismanaged, but that, as I also recall, was your doing, not Gibson's.'

'There were . . . difficulties,' said Maitland, meekly.

'No doubt there were.' Sir Nicholas's tone was dry, but his mind had already obviously left the matter. 'He will, I imagine, also be getting in touch with Miss Langhorne to act as your junior.'

'Vera? Well . . . no.'

'Is that your idea, or his?'

'I suppose . . . well, actually, I thought, Wellesley – '

'As Miss Langhorne has been associated with you on no fewer than three occasions in the past – '

'Yes, but this time – '

'Well?' He waited and then, as no answer was forthcoming, added in his most dulcet tone, 'You were going to tell me, were you not, that this time, in view of the danger involved, you did not propose to call upon her assistance?'

Antony hesitated. His first instinct was to deny everything, but with Uncle Nick what use was that? 'I suppose,' he said carefully, 'that something of the sort had crossed my mind.'

'I thought as much. Then you will agree with me, Antony, that all this – this poppycock about treating the brief on its merits and not meddling any further in your client's affairs, was designed with the sole purpose of misleading me.'

'No, I meant it. It's only that . . . there's always the possibility that things may get out of hand.'

Sir Nicholas regarded him in silence for a moment. 'I believe you mean what you say,' he said then, grudgingly. 'But you must admit that where your affairs are concerned – '

'Nothing to do with me,' said Antony quickly. 'Fate,' he added, in a hopeful tone.

Sir Nicholas laughed. 'Dell, I'm glad you are being at least partially honest with me,' he said. 'All the same, I think you must reconsider your decision not to work with Vera Langhorne.'

'But, Uncle Nick – '

'If it will salve your conscience you may explain to her, as you have to me under pressure, that there is some risk involved. At least that way the decision will be hers. If you make it for her, arbitrarily and without explanation, I think you will hurt her badly. She is a sensitive woman . . . something you may not have realised.'

'Of course I know that.' Maitland was inclined to be indignant. As his uncle had reminded him, he had worked with Vera Langhorne several times in the past, and she was one of the people that he and Jenny always kept in touch with; by this time he considered he knew her very well indeed. 'I'll ask Mallory to get in touch with Gibson in the morning, and then have a word with Vera myself.'

'I'm sure that will be the best thing.' Sir Nicholas, having got his way, was inclined to amiability. 'Have you any idea when the case will be heard?'

'Sometime next week, in all probability. At least, that's what Sykes thought.'

'Do you realise that this will probably be the last summer assize to be held in Northdean . . . or anywhere else for that matter?'

'I hadn't thought about it.' (That's done it. Dispose of one grievance, and another rears its head.)

'I must admit,' said Sir Nicholas, for perhaps the fiftieth time since the matter was first mooted, 'that I have the gravest misgivings about these new Crown Courts. You will admit, Antony, that I have never been in favour of change for change's sake . . .'

II

Half an hour later, having with some nobility refused the offer of his uncle's excellent cognac in favour of having a much inferior nightcap with Jenny, Antony left the study, crossed the hall, and went upstairs to his own quarters. The house had been divided immediately after the war, as a temporary expedient, and with the intention of giving the Maitlands some privacy; it was many years now since there had been any talk of their moving, and all the rules and regulations that had been originally laid down to ensure the smooth running of a two-family establishment had long ago been forgotten.

Jenny Maitland was waiting for him in the living-room. Perhaps it was that room more than any other – though the bedroom was of a good size too – that had ensured the permanence of their residence in Kempenfeldt Square. It was a big room, and none of the furniture matched, and the sofa was not a thing of beauty, though supremely comfortable; but there was a fire in the grate against the chill of that May evening, Jenny had made new curtains not more than a month before, there were flowers, and there were books, and there was an undeniable air of tranquillity. Antony always savoured this in the moment of homecoming, even when, as now, he had only been downstairs for an hour with his uncle, but it was Jenny's temperament that the room reflected, not – he would have admitted – his own.

Jenny took one look at his face as he crossed the room towards the fireplace. 'Uncle Nick's being awkward,' she said positively. Antony smiled at her and took up his favourite position in front of the fireplace, a little to one side of the grate and with one shoulder leaning against the high mantel, before he replied.

'Not more so than usual,' he said then. 'He's ordered me to specify Vera as my junior.'

'But of course you'll have Vera,' said Jenny, surprised. 'Why on earth shouldn't you?'

It wasn't the first time the room's peacefulness had betrayed him into saying more than he should for Jenny's peace of mind. Now he tried to retrieve the position. 'No reason at all,' he said hurriedly. 'That's what I'm going to do.'

'Have you talked to her yet?'

'Not yet.'

'Why don't you ring her now?'

'Tomorrow.'

'But – '

'It's getting late, love.'

'It's only a quarter past ten,' Jenny objected. 'And you know Vera always stays up late listening to her records.'

'Well, I don't want to disturb her.'

Obligingly, Jenny dropped the subject, but she had a dissatisfied air. 'When do you have to go to Northdean?' she asked.

'Next week. Perhaps I shall even have to travel up on Sunday night. I want time to go over things thoroughly with Gibson before the case comes on.' But the subject was distasteful, he was uneasy with it, and Jenny was altogether too perceptive for his comfort at the moment. 'Uncle Nick takes the dimmest view of the new Crown Courts,' he told her. 'I just hope he won't bore you stiff with the subject while I'm away.'

SUNDAY, 23rd MAY

Northdean is the county town, the county being West-hampton. It is a grey, solid place that still centres round its market square, though there is a bus terminal there now instead of cattle pens, and the market is held in a more convenient location on the outskirts. There is some industry on the outskirts too, and the town boasts a number of good shops, and the Red Lion – the hostelry where the Bar Mess is generally established during an assize – has a degree of comfort, and even a certain mild sophistication, that Maitland regarded with favour when he arrived there rather late in the evening and the porter showed him to his room. It was a little larger than the one he had occupied on his previous visit, but equally comfortable.

He couldn't complain about the journey; the train had been fast and comfortable, and had even provided him with a reasonable meal. But before he left there had been a conference, held on the Sunday because he might be away all the week; an extremely trying conference as it turned out, with a client far too glib, far too talkative for his own good. Now he had to admit he was tired and the ache in his shoulder, a legacy of the war, was more insistent than usual.

But still, there was the message: ask Mr. Maitland to phone Mr. Gibson when he gets in, and the appropriate number considerately appended. No mention of the possibility of the train being late, and of course it hadn't been. In any event, he knew the solicitor well enough to know he'd be waiting for the call, whatever time of the night it might be put through.

It was Lucy Gibson who answered when he rang, which

14

he'd been rather dreading because he wasn't by any means sure of his reception in that quarter. But all was well. There was cordiality in her tone, and something more that might have been relief. 'I wanted to talk to you, Mr. Maitland,' she said, as soon as she had greeted him. 'Peter's worried about this case.'

No good saying, That's what he's paid for. Taking the easy way out, 'I'm sorry to hear that,' said Antony cautiously. 'But I don't know much about it yet, you see.'

'No, of course not. Peter will tell you. But I don't want you to be put off by Philip Brady's manner; he isn't always very wise, but he's nice really, and quite a friend of ours.'

'I see.' And he thought he did, only too well. If anything had been needed to make the situation more difficult . . . 'You know we shall do our best for him, Mrs. Gibson.'

'Of course I do. You must come to dinner, Mr. Maitland. Could you manage tomorrow night?'

He couldn't think of any excuse, wasn't even sure that he wished to make one. The worst he knew of Peter Gibson was that he was conscientious, and of Lucy that she was perhaps over-kind and that she liked sweet sherry. Why hesitate, then, when he liked them both, and they seemed willing to let bygones be bygones? 'That would be very pleasant,' he said. 'I should be glad to come.'

'All right then. Peter's getting impatient. Here you are.'

'Thank you.' He didn't think she heard that, Gibson was already speaking. After nearly six years he couldn't have recognised Lucy's voice, but Peter's was immediately familiar.

'Sorry to bother you at this time of night,' he was saying. 'I thought we'd better fix up about tomorrow.'

'Any time you say.'

'Ten o'clock, then. Will you come to the office? We're in Westgate Street, number 59. Turn left when you leave the hotel.'

'Right.'

'Vera will be there. She's coming over from Chedcombe.'

He wasn't quite sure whether that was a threat or a promise. He knew Vera liked him, and trusted him . . . up to a point. But there could be difficulties. However, Gibson wasn't likely to know anything about that. 'Good,' he said. 'I expect she's as much in the dark as I am.'

'If you'd read your brief – ' Peter began. Antony grinned at the telephone; it wasn't the first time that had been said to him.

'I read it all right,' he protested. 'But you must admit there are points that will be better elucidated in person.'

'Yes, I suppose so. Anyway, I'm glad you could take the case.'

To reply in kind to that would be an outright lie. 'I shall be glad to see you and Mrs. Gibson again,' said Antony, skirting the question rather neatly, he thought.

'Tomorrow then.' Gibson sounded amused, perhaps the evasion had been more obvious than he had intended. 'I won't keep you up any longer tonight.'

He talked to Jenny for a few minutes after that, and then got ready for bed. The window was already open, the weather had turned warm suddenly, but he went and pushed it wider, rather clumsily, taking the weight on his left hand. He placed his book, a new one by Jeremy Skelton, on the bedside table, and was just in the act of stripping off the heavy counterpane when the phone rang.

He stood and looked at it for a moment, without making any attempt to pick up the receiver, and was conscious of a feeling of time returned. It might be Jenny, with something she had forgotten to say; it might be Sir Nicholas, though that was unlikely: he wasn't given to second thoughts, and anything he wanted to communicate would have been taken care of before he left home; it might even be Peter Gibson, though that too was unlikely in view of the very definite arrangement they had made for the next day. And then it struck him that it might be Vera Langhorne, and he had picked up the receiver and said, 'Hallo' before it occurred to him that even the cost of the call from Chedcombe might well be a consideration to her, when she couldn't have anything more useful to say than Welcome.

And, as he had half expected, he was greeted only by silence. He said, 'Hallo' again, but without any expectation of being answered, and then, after a moment's hesitation, 'Maitland here.' And at that the connection was very gently broken, but the click as the receiver was replaced at the other end of the line was distinct enough to convince him that there had, in fact, been someone there.

So . . . 'they' knew he was here, and wouldn't be in any doubt as to the reason. Last week when he talked to his uncle he had been quite sincere in saying that he didn't expect any repercussions from taking the case; all the same he knew now that subconsciously he must have been aware of the pitfalls that might be lying in wait for him. But if the man he had called, half in mockery, Mr. X knew already that he was in Northdean, and true to form had caused him to be telephoned for confirmation . . . because that was what he had done last time . . .

Well, now he knew. And he could guess, I suppose, as easily as Uncle Nick did, that I may be tempted to meddle. Because I have to confess to a prejudice, not quite unjustified, in my client's favour. 'I have made it my business to know a good deal about you, Mr. Maitland.' That was what Mr. X had said, or something very like it, when we finally came face to face. And still I didn't . . . don't . . . know who he is. Not that I want to, none of my business. And what the hell concern of his is it that two of his minions got into trouble in Northdean? They don't know who he is either, you can take a bet on that.

He realised suddenly that there was a cool breeze coming through the window now, finished his job of pulling off the counterpane and draping it across a chair, and climbed into bed. It was no use worrying; probably the chap would realise sooner or later that he had no intention of going beyond his brief.

But what if he didn't?

MONDAY, 24th MAY

I

The next morning it was as warm as midsummer. Maitland breakfasted in a leisurely way, with the *Northdean Daily Record* propped up against the coffee pot, and read without much interest that elections had been held in Trinidad which resulted in a fourth term in office for the Prime Minister, and that the Soviet President had arrived in Egypt 'for talks'. Sometimes it seemed to him that altogether too much talking went on in the world, but if you were to say that, you had to admit, too, that lawyers were responsible for a good deal of it. He drank the last of his coffee, abandoned the paper without regret, and went out into the sunshine.

Westgate Street was familiar ground to him, he had walked its length before. This time, however, he found the offices of Noyes and Gibson, Solicitors and Commissioners for Oaths, on the left-hand side before he had proceeded more than a couple of hundred yards from the square. There was a good deal of traffic about and he was glad enough to turn into the building and climb, as a painted finger directed, to the first floor. And once there he felt completely at home, the very smell of the place – the dusty smell of long-undisturbed parchment – was familiar. There was a placid middle-aged woman, and a harassed-looking girl, and a youth who seemed to be trying, not very successfully, to balance the petty cash. There were bundles of deeds everywhere, as though the strong-room had finally reached saturation point and overflowed over the outer office. There was a Will being typed, and what looked like a Conveyance, but when he asked for Mr. Gibson and mentioned the time of his appointment all three of them stopped work and looked at him.

Finally the older woman said, 'You must be Mr. Maitland.' And added, getting to her feet, 'I'll show you Mr. Gibson's room.'

Peter Gibson's office was a pleasant, if rather conventional, room, and comparatively free from the clutter that prevailed elsewhere. Vera Langhorne was there already, drinking coffee, and Antony thought, as she surged from her chair to greet him, how little she changed with the passing years. She must be turned sixty now, a tall, rather heavily-built woman with thick, untidy hair that had once been dark but now had a good deal of grey in it. A shabby raincoat that he was sure must be hers was thrown over a chair, and the sack-like garment she wore might easily be the very dress she had on when last he saw her. He thought too, and was surprised by the thought, that bright colours might suit her, it was a pity she always insisted on wearing what are known as neutral shades.

In spite of his previous misgivings, there could be no doubt that she was pleased to see him. Peter Gibson, observing them benignly, had an amused look. He, too, was tall, as tall as Maitland perhaps, and more than usually thin. Mid-forties now? Pale blue eyes, and hair that was fairish and straight. 'Been telling him,' said Vera, with a gesture in his direction, 'good idea to get you in on this.'

Well, he had warned her, and if she chose to disregard his remarks as though they had never been made there was no use dragging up the subject again. Not to be outdone in the exchange of courtesies he said with a touch of formality, 'I'm glad to have the opportunity of working with you again.' And then, turning to Peter, 'At least, between us, we have a little background knowledge of diamond smuggling.' That wasn't the most tactful reminder of their former association, but it was important to have things out in the open, to know how the other man felt.

'So we do.' Gibson sounded thoughtful, but went on after only a moment's pause, as though he guessed Maitland's thought, 'It seems a long time ago now. I expect it's seemed an age to Alan.' (Alan Barnard was his brother-in-law, and if anybody other than himself could be blamed for his prison term it was Antony Maitland.) 'Another two or three years, though, and he may be getting out.'

'Yes, I suppose so. How is Mrs. Gibson?'

'She doesn'. blame you, you know,' said Peter, answering the spirit rather than the letter of the question. He seemed to be in a mood for plain speaking, which pleased Antony in a way, but also alarmed him. 'In fact, we're both looking forward to this evening. Could you stay and have dinner with us too, Miss Langhorne?'

'Better get back,' said Vera. As usual, she sounded gruff, but this did not disguise her pleasure in the invitation. 'Have to stay here when the case starts, of course, but rather not until I have to.'

'No, I see. Sit down, both of you.' Gibson went back to his chair behind the desk again. 'Now then, what do you want to know?'

'Everything,' said Maitland comprehensively. Vera said nothing, but smiled her rather grim smile and nodded her head.

The demand did not seem to disturb Gibson overmuch. He said, quite seriously, 'At least, you know our client's name.'

'Philip Brady,' said Maitland promptly. 'He's a Detective Inspector in the local C.I.D., and was the principal witness against the plaintiffs when they were tried for diamond smuggling. You see,' he added, 'I did read my brief.'

'It gave you a few facts other than that.'

'But I'd much rather hear them from you. Then if there's anything to discuss Miss Langhorne and I can chip in.'

'All right. The trial was during the Winter Assize, the beginning of February if I remember rightly. Wellesley was prosecuting – '

'Why the devil didn't you get him to take on this matter then?'

'I thought, a change of perspective – ' Peter shrugged.

'Anyway, he hadn't been conspicuously successful the first time around.'

'That could hardly be said to be his fault. As I understand it, none of his witnesses came up to proof.'

'That's perfectly true.'

'This change of perspective you talk about – '

'I always thought you could see further through a brick wall than most.'

Maitland laughed at that. 'My uncle puts it rather less politely,' he said, but before he could amplify the statement he was interrupted by Vera, who said firmly.

'Like to point out, not getting us any further with the briefing.'

Antony was immediately contrite. 'My fault,' he said. 'Only I couldn't help wondering – ' He broke off there, with an apologetic look in Miss Langhorne's direction. 'Let's get back to Detective Inspector Philip Brady.'

This time it was Peter Gibson's turn to digress. 'He doesn't like barristers much,' he said. 'The defence chap gave him a bad time in court.'

So that was why Lucy had warned him. There was nothing for it but to meet that problem when it arose. 'We must try to make him change his mind,' said Antony. 'Meanwhile – '

'He tells me he thought the case was all cut and dried,' Gibson went on, and Maitland made a mental note that the way he put it might mean something. Or then again, it mightn't. 'It all started with a man in New York who found a diamond in a pot of Westhampton cheese, which surprised him rather – '

'I should think it might.'

' – and when he'd thought about it a bit he went to the police. They investigated, of course. The cheese had been bought from a delicatessen shop which specialises in imported foods, and had been sent to them by a Northdean firm, Hargreaves & Company.'

'I've had it when I was here before, I think. Not unlike Stilton, but a bit more creamy in colour.'

'That's right. For export they put it up in these little earthenware pots, and the customs people waited until the next consignment came in and then made a thorough search. Got quite a haul, as I understand it. The pots with diamonds in were specially marked, a fault in the printing on the label ostensibly. Somehow the one sold to the honest New Yorker had got the wrong label on it.'

'Ingenious,' said Vera.

'And I suppose when the American police, or customs, or whatever, got in touch with the Northdean force *they* directed their attention to Hargreaves & Company,' Maitland put in.

'They did. But covertly at first.'

'Wanting to catch somebody red-handed, rather than just scare the culprits off. Very reasonable, from their point of view.'

'I suppose so. And I may as well tell you straight away, they never found out where the faulty labels came from. Apart from that, the first thing they turned their attention to was the Packing Department . . . three men and a supervisor, so it didn't present too much of a problem. They put tails on all of them, and before long it was noticed that the supervisor, John Irving, was having regular meetings in the bar at the Red Lion with another employee of the firm, Clifford Dobell, the Export Manager.'

'I'm staying at the Red Lion,' said Antony, rather as though this fact rendered what he was being told improbable.

'So you are. You probably know the barman then, a chap called Noyes.'

'No. No, I don't think so. What drinking I've done there has generally been in the Bar Mess,' Maitland told him.

'Well, it doesn't matter. You'll see him in court,' Gibson promised, but not as though he derived much satisfaction from the thought. 'Philip says . . . Lucy did explain to you that we know him rather well, didn't she?'

'Yes, I understand that.'

'Well, he says he talked to Noyes and Noyes told him that

the two men were often in there together, and that he had seen small packages pass between them on more than one occasion.'

'Dobell to Irving, or Irving to Dobell?'

'The former. So naturally Philip began to think that Dobell was getting hold of illicit diamonds somehow, and passing them to Irving to pack and send out of the country. The next thing he did was question the three other men in the Packing Department . . . at their homes, of course, not at work. And he got the same story from each of them, there were occasions when Irving stayed on overtime, alone. One of them said he'd offered to stay and help on several occasions, and been refused.'

'Didn't he think that rather odd?'

'No. Old Mr. Hargreaves, who is the Managing Director – it's a private firm – disapproves of overtime, says it shouldn't be necessary. So the packer just thought Irving preferred to do the work himself, rather than get into an argument with the management. But, when pressed, he said he thought he could find out some dates and what was being shipped the following day, and what he came up with made interesting reading when Philip wrote it down. Whenever an order was to be shipped to the delicatessen I mentioned, in New York, Irving had worked late the evening before. Other overtime preceded shipments to Antwerp and Munich, though I admit I don't quite see why they can't get their stones direct from Africa, if they want to deal in the illicit market.'

'It's all part of a process of covering their tracks; Chief Inspector Sykes explained it all to me when we were mixed up in that business before.'

'Like to have it explained to *me*,' said Vera.

'I'll try. He said the rewards are enormous, I remember that, and while the armaments race continues he didn't think you'd ever wipe the traffic out. The final destination is usually Russia, or China. I queried that, because the Russians are said to have their own fields, but he said all he knew was that

23

they were certainly stock-piling industrial stones from this side of the Iron Curtain. He said a few illegal sales were made in the States, too, but it seemed to be more profitable to sell to the communists.'

'So the Antwerp and Munich shipments – ?'

'Were probably going to them. Sykes said they'd be dispersed first, after the original theft in Africa, to any one of half a dozen places – Italy, Belgium, England – then the stones would be brought together at some central point – Holland, perhaps, or Germany – and from there they'd make the last part of the journey. That would be the easiest part, there'd be no question of smuggling any longer . . . the government concerned would be only too eager to get their hands on them.'

'That all fits in with what little we know, doesn't it?'

'It does. But there's more to it than that. You'll gather the police know a good deal about the trade, which Sykes says is highly organised. But there's the little matter of proof, as we know only too well. They occasionally catch one of the minor characters, as Evans was caught in the Barnard trial, but they never – I'm still quoting Sykes – get near the men at the top.'

'Talking of Evans – ' said Peter Gibson. He broke off there and glanced at Vera, and then back at Maitland again, as though wondering how they would take what he was about to say. 'Talking of Evans,' he repeated firmly, 'he incriminated himself at the trial, and he said it was out of concern for Camilla. I never believed that, somehow. How did you arrange it?'

'I did a deal with the man at the top, and he made it worth Evans's while, I suppose.'

'Then you know who – '

'Unfortunately, no. Even Uncle Nick is reduced to calling him Mr. X, which offends him, as you can imagine.'

'I don't see – '

'No, of course you don't. I told Miss Langhorne about it at the time, but considering what else happened at Camilla's

24

trial it didn't seem tactful to insist on seeing you and going into the whole affair.'

'I can understand *that*,' said Gibson, a little dryly.

'I'm sure you can. But I'd better explain, I suppose. I angled for an invitation to meet Mr. X by getting a friend of mine to leak to the press the fact that I was interesting myself unofficially in the case. And when Uncle Nick got going in court and it became obvious to anyone in the know that he was proposing to establish, if he could, the firm's connection with the trade in illicit diamonds, Mr. X came to the conclusion it might be as well to see me. He sent a chap he called a courier to fetch me, and the journey was made in a car – a Rolls-Royce, no less – with all the blinds firmly drawn.'

'Weren't you afraid it might be a one way trip?' asked Peter curiously. And Vera interjected the one word,

'Foolhardy,' into the conversation.

Antony smiled at her. 'I'm afraid so,' he admitted. 'But I managed to persuade him, you see, that his precious organisation might be imperilled if Uncle Nick continued on that course. It was better to throw Alan Barnard – and Evans, of course – to the wolves and have the questions stop short at his implication in the trade.'

'But haven't you any clue to his identity, this Mr. X you talk about?' Gibson succeeded in sounding faintly aggrieved.

'I should recognise him again, of course, but he assured me that he never allows himself to be photographed; so short of bumping into him by chance in the street that's not much good. I don't know the street his house is in, only that it's number 10. I made some crack about that, wondering if I should find myself at a cabinet meeting, and he informed me quite seriously – I think I can remember his exact words – that "though the gentleman in Downing Street is better known that I am, he is a good deal less influential".'

'Then all this doesn't really help, does it?' said Gibson glumly.

'Know what we're up against,' said Vera flatly.

'You're assuming, then, that the same organisation is involved?' Peter was looking at Miss Langhorne as he spoke, but it was Maitland who answered.

'It would be a coincidence, surely, if another racket on the same lines had grown up independently in Northdean.' To his mind, the unfinished phone call last night clinched the matter, but for some reason or another he didn't feel prepared at that moment to go into that.

Perhaps Vera sensed this. 'Where were we when we digressed?' she wondered.

'Peter was outlining the case against Dobell and Irving.' It was characteristic of Maitland that, however far he might digress, he never altogether lost sight of the point of a discussion. 'We'd got to the evidence of one of the packers who'd looked at the firm's records to see when Irving worked overtime.'

'I may have misled you a little about that. He was relying on his memory about those dates; I told you old Mr. Hargreaves doesn't approve of overtime. None was paid, and no records were kept. But there were records, of course, of the firm's shipments.'

'I see.'

'You will in a minute,' Gibson promised. 'By this time Philip was beginning to think he had a case, so he got search warrants. That wasn't too popular a move, Mr. Hargreaves was vocal about police persecution, but after all diamonds had been found in products shipped by them. And then, of course, nothing was found on the firm's premises, so he complained more than ever.'

'But presumably that wasn't the only search that was made,' said Maitland thoughtfully.

'No, it was quite a big operation. Dobell's and Irving's houses were done simultaneously with the cheese factory. And in Dobell's den – that's what he insists on calling it – they found five rather magnificent uncut diamonds.'

'Now we're getting somewhere.'

'That's just what Philip thought. And then they took the case to court and the whole thing disintegrated.'

'Don't quite see – ' said Miss Langhorne. For such a downright person she was oddly diffident about interrupting.

Gibson didn't point out, as he certainly would have done if Maitland had spoken, that it was all in the brief. Instead he continued his patient explanation. 'What happened, you see, was that one witness after another got up and completely contradicted everything they'd said before. Noyes, the barman, said he knew both men but couldn't recollect ever having seen them together; Carter, the packer I spoke of, didn't remember any dates, so there was nothing to connect Irving with any particular shipment; and last but not least the defence produced a Bristol jeweller, by the name of Marston, who said Dobell had purchased the diamonds from him some weeks before, a perfectly regular transaction.'

'Wait a bit – '

'It looked, of course, as if Philip – who gave his evidence first in the firm conviction that the witnesses would back him up – had invented the whole thing.'

'But surely the records – '

'If you mean Hargreaves & Company's record of the shipments, they didn't mean a thing when the prosecution could no longer tie Irving to them, or Dobell to Irving.'

'The statements then. The witnesses had made statements to the police.'

'Yes, of course. This is the queerest thing of all,' said Peter, looking from one to the other of his audience. 'Somewhere or other along the line the statements had disappeared.'

'Oh, come now! There'd be the copies sent with Wellesley's brief, and at least one set in the police files too.'

'Wellesley's copies were there when he worked on the brief, and had disappeared when the papers were put together to go to court. When he demanded duplicates from the office of the Director of Public Prosecutions, they couldn't produce them either. And neither, it turned out, could the police.'

'But . . . good lord! That's organisation on a massive

27

scale. Had any of the people responsible any explanation to offer?'

'In no case had there been any obvious breaking in. There must have been three seperate inside jobs, Antony, and you can see that was rather a lot to get the jury to swallow.'

'Yes, I can see that, but surely – '

'There was a rumpus, of course, but that was all outside the court.'

'I'll have to talk to Wellesley, and anybody else who can fill me in. Or have you done that already?'

'No, I thought you'd rather. I doubt if there's much to be got from any of them though.'

'The statements didn't go missing by accident,' said Maitland flatly.

'Of course not, but it would be the devil and all to prove. And as if all that wasn't bad enough,' said Gibson gloomily, 'both the defendants made noises about undue pressure from the police in taking *their* statements. As the jury already thought Philip was lying, I expect they were inclined to believe that too.'

'Defendants hadn't admitted anything,' Vera put in. Maitland turned to her and smiled.

'No, but I can see what Peter means. There's one thing, though, the chap who took down the statements . . . Brady wasn't alone when he interviewed these people.'

'Constable Peach was called, of course, when it was obvious how things were going, but his evidence was put down to collaboration, I expect. There was some talk of calling the constables who'd shadowed Dobell and Irving, but – for the same reason, I suppose – Wellesley didn't think much of that idea. Anyway, nothing did any good. The defence called the two accused in turn, and then Marston, and after that the judge dismissed the case without putting it to the jury at all.'

'Wasn't there anything to be done with Marston's evidence? I can see it took the police by surprise, but surely – '

'It would have been too late anyway. But as it turned out everything looked to be in order. It wasn't the first time Dobell had bought diamonds from Marston, they were his form of investment.'

'We'll have to go into it a bit further than that. How was payment made? What about Dobell's bank account?'

'We haven't a hope of getting a sight of that.'

'I suppose not. But we can ask Marston questions when we get him into the witness box. What do you think, Miss Langhorne? We can make it awkward for him at least.'

Vera gave that her consideration. 'Leave that kind of thing to you,' she said at last.

'I don't want to put a damper on your enthusiasm, Antony,' Gibson put in. 'But I'd be willing to bet all that has been covered. They'd never have brought the action – '

'Yes, why have they brought it?'

'The obvious reason is spite.'

'No, I think there must be more to it than that. There are still the diamonds being shipped from Hargreaves's cheese factory to be accounted for. Perhaps this action is to discourage any further investigation by the police.'

'But – '

'The shipments containing diamonds will quietly stop, of course, but somebody might still find it embarrassing. Well, you've presented us with a nice can of worms, Peter.' His tone was reproachful, but he was smiling as he spoke. 'Let's see what we think we can do with it. Miss Langhorne – '

Their discussion lasted the rest of the morning. They had only time for a hurried lunch before putting Vera on the bus back to Chedcombe. After that they were to talk to Detective Inspector Philip Brady, a meeting which Maitland found himself looking forward to with the liveliest curiosity. For the moment he had succeeded in putting the memory of the silent telephone call altogether out of his mind.

II

Inspector Brady had gone home to receive them. He was a man of no more than middle height, very dark of hair and complexion, and slightly built, but Maitland had the immediate feeling that he might be a good man to have beside you in a scrap. From the jut of his chin he might not be an unwilling participant, but the trouble was, if he started anything at the moment, it seemed extremely unlikely that he would be taking the part of his counsel. His tone was abrupt as he greeted them and added briefly, 'The room on the right.' It was a rather cramped apartment in a new building on the outskirts of Northdean, but it certainly wasn't over-furnished. What pieces there were, however, looked to have been carefully chosen, and the easy chairs in the room to which Brady had directed them probably lived up to their name.

Antony wasn't looking at them, however. He had followed Peter Gibson into the room which wasn't, as he had expected, unoccupied. There was a girl in the chair by the open window, and it didn't take a second glance to see that she was a very pretty girl indeed, with dark red hair that waved to her shoulders and had nothing at all of ginger in it. She had the creamy complexion of the true redhead, eyes that were intensely blue, and lips that might or might not owe their colour to nature but that were certainly warm and inviting. And if that was an odd thought to cross his mind in the first moments of their acquaintance, it might be because she was smiling at him.

Peter had come to a full stop, and Antony came up beside him. Philip Brady from the doorway was saying, 'Peter Gibson and Antony Maitland, Moira. My fiancée, Moira Pershing.' Now that he said more than the bare words of greeting it occurred to Antony that his voice wasn't any too steady.

Gibson seemed almost equally uneasy. As soon as the

greetings that politeness demanded had been exchanged he turned to Brady and said without preamble, 'You did understand, Philip – didn't you? – that Maitland wants to talk to you about the case.'

'Yes, of course.' Brady sounded surprised, which in itself might be considered odd. 'Oh, you mean because Moira is here. She said – '

'I wanted to meet the celebrated barrister from London.' Her voice was slightly husky, which somehow underlined the fact that she was laughing at him. 'You have quite a reputation in Northdean, Mr. Maitland. I've heard of you from friends in Chedcombe too.'

'Nothing good, I dare say.' Antony was trying for a light tone, but her remarks had ruffled him and he didn't altogether succeed in hiding the fact.

'This and that,' she told him airily. 'The man who never loses a case, for instance.' And then, still amused, 'Does it worry you? I thought lawyers learned not to be thin-skinned.'

'It's the absurdity – ' he began. But he had, after all, no need to explain himself . . . certainly not to her. 'Perhaps some of us don't learn it well enough,' he said, and in his turn looked at Brady. 'If you prefer it, of course, *we* – Mr. Gibson and I – have no objection to Miss Pershing sitting in on our talk, but – ' He broke off, eyeing Brady quizzically, and unexpectedly Philip laughed.

'You're going to bully me and you don't want a witness,' he said. For the moment he sounded almost good-humoured, but Antony doubted if his mood would last long once they got down to business.

'I'd rather put it that some of my questions may come rather near to the bone,' he said. He didn't think the note of apology in his tone deceived Brady for an instant. Nor, just then, did he greatly care.

'Well, in that case – ' Philip looked at the girl rather helplessly, and it was Peter's turn to look surprised. Antony found himself remembering the impression he had got from his conversation with Lucy Gibson, and later from her husband. It seemed almost as if their friend was deliberately setting out to prove them wrong in their estimation of his character. Perhaps it was time to jolt the chap a little.

'In that case,' he said, 'I think we should all find it easier . . . and less distracting . . . if Miss Pershing were to leave us. Unless, of course,' – he glanced from Philip to Moira, and then back to his client again – 'you find yourselves in such perfect harmony as to have no secrets from each other at all.'

Moira got up. It was a graceful movement and, with the couple of inches' advantage that her heels gave her, brought her eyes almost level with Brady's. 'I don't aspire to perfection,' she said, 'but you might as well say straight out that I'm in the way.' She stooped to retrieve her handbag, which had been beside her in the chair. 'However, I've no wish to stay . . . really.' She began to stroll towards the door, not hurrying herself. 'Goodbye, Mr. Maitland, Mr. Gibson. I'll see you this evening, Philip.' She paused there, to kiss Brady in a businesslike way; a moment later the front door closed behind her.

Philip came forward into the room. 'Having got what you want, Mr. Maitland,' he said, 'we may as well sit down.' He waited until they had followed this advice, and then seated himself in the chair by the window that Moira's departure had left vacant. 'What are these rather frightening questions of yours?' he asked. 'Or were you just trying to make my flesh creep?' He was making a good effort to appear light-hearted, but it didn't altogether come off.

'Well, to begin with,' said Antony, who had meant to start the interview cautiously but now seemed to be committed to a tougher line in the effort to take his client's measure, 'I'd like to know whether you really did frame Dobell and Irving.'

The question left a stillness in the room. He heard Peter catch his breath, and then Brady said, his voice completely expressionless, 'I'm your client . . . remember?'

'I hadn't forgotten, but if I'm to help you – '

'All right then!' There was anger in his tone, but still he

wasn't reacting quite as violently as Maitland had expected. 'We built up a perfectly genuine case, step by step. There was nothing phoney about it.'

'It was rather odd that none of the witnesses came up to proof . . . don't you think?'

'Very odd,' Brady agreed harshly.

'And even more strange that their statements – the statements they had allegedly made – should have disappeared.'

'I can't explain it.' Now Brady sounded merely bewildered. 'But Peach will back me up that the statements were taken and signed in due form; and Wellesley, of course, can say that they were at one time in his possession.'

'Come now, you know better than that. The plaintiffs will say Constable Peach was your accomplice; and though Wellesley knows that he had at one time some documents in his possession he can't swear to the signatures. And in the absence of the statements you can't prove the signatures were genuine.'

'No, I see that. But . . . forget about my integrity for a moment. My *alleged* integrity,' he interpolated bitterly, and Antony felt the first, unwelcome stirring of sympathy for the other man's predicament. 'Would I have been fool enough to put on a case that I couldn't possible substantiate?'

'That's a point I can appreciate, but I wonder if the jury will. By the time they've heard Dobell and Irving tell how you browbeat them . . . what do your colleagues here in Northdean think about all this?' he added, turning the subject abruptly.

'*They* believe me.' The emphasis was faint, but revealing. Antony smiled at him.

'Yes, I gathered as much from Sykes. Now, the witnesses we can't do anything about until we get into court. Unless . . . the barman and the chap from the Packing Department. Are the plaintiffs calling them?' He turned to look at Peter Gibson as he spoke.

'They are. It's part of their case, of course, that the statements were forgeries, so they have to call all the witnesses

33

who are alleged to have made them, so that they can deny it. And I'm using the word without prejudice, Philip,' he added. 'It doesn't mean I don't believe you.' (And even that might be equivocation, Maitland thought. He'd very much like to know Gibson's honest opinion.)

Brady made no answer to that. His eyes were fixed on counsel's face. 'On the whole I think that's a good thing,' said Maitland reflectively. 'If we can break them down in cross-examination – '

'I don't want to discourage you,' Gibson told him, very much as he had done earlier in the day, 'but I don't think you have a hope of doing that. They were very positive, and Wellesley did his best to shift them, of course. Besides, if you're right and your Mr. X is behind everything, there were probably threats used as well as bribery.'

'I'm sorry to say that I agree with you, but at least we can try. The other line that may repay enquiry – '

'I don't understand,' said Brady, interrupting him. 'Mr. X? It sounds like a bad movie.'

'I'll explain Mr. X to you presently,' said Maitland, 'on condition you keep your own counsel about what I tell you.'

'That sounds . . . almost . . . as if you trusted me,' said Brady. His tone was oddly tentative. For answer, Antony only smiled at him again.

'It's more immediately important to decide on a plan of action.' He looked from one of his companions to the other. 'As I told you, Peter, I can see Wellesley; I can talk to somebody – to several somebodies, I hope – from the D.D.P.'s office. But I expect you, Mr. Brady, are as good a source as anyone for what happened at the police station.'

'About the missing statements?'

'Exactly. To begin with, have you any ideas on the subject?'

'If you mean who could have done it, no, I haven't. It seems incredible – '

'Incredible or not, it happened. I don't believe that three sets of the same documents went missing by accident.'

'No, of course not, but – '

'So if you have any ideas on the subject, let's have them.'

'I don't. I told you.' He seemed about to leave it there, and Antony said, still rather impatiently,

'There's obviously *something* you can tell us. For instance, where were the statements kept?'

'We're rather short of space. The old filing room is now Inspector Mawson's office and the cabinets are distributed about the place. Not a particularly convenient arrangement, I'm afraid.'

'These particular documents – '

'Were in my office.'

'I don't much like the sound of that.' (And Brady knew what it sounded like, he'd be a fool if he didn't. And that, in spite of his obvious disinclination completely to trust his counsel, Maitland very much doubted.)

'I didn't think you would,' Brady retorted.

'Was the cabinet locked?'

'Yes, of course. And I don't have the key.'

'Who has?'

'Sergeant Cummings. He's in charge of' – he waved his hand vaguely – 'all that sort of thing.'

'What did he have to say about it?'

'The key hadn't been out of his possession.'

'Did he qualify that statement in any way?'

'No, he seemed very sure of the fact.'

'About the filing cabinet then. Was it one of those with a special locking device, the kind that are used for secret documents?'

'There was nothing very special about it. There's a thing you push, and that locks it. I suppose that its being located in the station was regarded as being sufficient protection.'

'Could it have been tampered with?'

'There was no sign of that.'

'Do you trust Sergeant Cummings?'

Brady hesitated over that. 'It never occurred to me not to,' he replied at last.

'The spare key, then. There must be one surely. If Cummings is ill, or loses his key-ring – '

'There is a spare, but it's not much help to us. It's kept in the safe in Superintendent Harley's room.'

'Then the same question about keys arises.'

'The Super has one that he carries, and the spare he keeps at home but I don't know where. I'm not going to be awfully popular if you start questioning all these people, you know.'

'I know, and I'm sorry. But I don't see how we can avoid it, do you?'

'I suppose not, but do you really think – ?'

'Never theorise ahead of your data, Peter will tell you that. Somebody removed those statements and it seems most likely . . . have you any idea when the theft took place, by the way?'

'Not really. They were there when the papers were sent to the D.P.P. and gone when I wanted to refresh my memory about them just before the trial.'

'Well, I'm not altogether satisfied as to that filing cabinet's impregnability if somebody set their mind to opening it without leaving traces; but even so it doesn't seem likely that an outsider could have got at it. So there'll be questions to ask, you'll just have to face up to it.'

Brady had a grimace for that. 'Yes, I know, but it's hard to believe – '

'I never expected to hear that from a member of the police force. I thought you were as disillusioned a bunch as lawyers are.'

It was Brady's turn to smile, perhaps at the resignation in the other man's tone. 'In general, I think that's true. But when it comes to one's colleagues – '

'Someone took the statements,' said Maitland flatly. 'I don't think it was an outsider, but I may be wrong.' He paused, frowning, and then went on briskly. 'Who lives may learn. Meanwhile, Peter, how long have we got before the case comes on?'

36

'Tomorrow, I should think, and probably most of Wednesday. It's fairly high in the list.'

'I see.'

'Where do you want to start?'

'I'll try and see Wellesley this afternoon; he's probably at the Red Lion already. I mean, besides our needing him he's fairly active on this circuit, isn't he? And the assize starts tomorrow.' He thought about that for a moment and then said in an amused tone, 'I find your attitude not so unreasonable after all, Mr. Brady. Wellesley's a friend of mine, I don't suspect him personally of the theft.'

Brady had nothing to say to that. Peter Gibson said into the silence, 'He'll be here tomorrow at the latest. I don't know what his commitments are, of course, but we need him as a witness.'

'A witness to the fact that the statements existed, even though the plaintiffs will say I wrote them myself,' said Brady glumly. He hadn't been in good spirits when the interview began, but now he sounded in the depths.

'Yes, well . . . look here, we'll do what we can with this, Peter and I,' said Maitland abruptly. 'It isn't quite time to despair yet.'

'I know.' That was said with an obvious effort at a more cheerful tone. 'I don't want you to think I don't appreciate – '

'Never mind that. We won't keep you much longer, but before we break up I'd like to go over your interviews with Dobell and Irving. Just for the record,' he added, and heard a conciliatory note in his own voice, and wondered at it.

III

But, after all, Wellesley hadn't arrived yet at the Red Lion. Antony had tea sent up to his room and worked on his brief with a diligence that would have gratified his instructing solicitor if Gibson could have seen it. And so, of course, the time passed more quickly than he realised, and he found himself already a little late when he rang down to the desk to ask for a cab to be called to take him to the Gibsons' home.

And everything there was just as he had remembered it, a large, untidy, cheerful house. Come to think of it, that wasn't a bad description of Lucy Gibson either; whatever she had been doing in the years since they met, she hadn't been slimming. She was a pleasant-looking woman with dark hair rather too carefully waved – a contrast to the loose gown she wore – that showed a touch of auburn in the lamplight. She greeted him as kindly, as maternally, as ever, and waved his apologies for tardiness aside. As an old friend, in fact . . . as though the events of six years ago had never taken place. But for all that he didn't make the mistake of thinking her insensitive. Such tears as she shed would be shed in private.

For a few minutes she fussed over his comfort, making sure he took the chair she selected for him, which was certainly a very comfortable one. 'I remember you prefer sherry,' she said then, not giving him a chance of avoiding the rather sweet brand she favoured. But somehow it didn't matter; anything else would have seemed inappropriate.

And tonight, perhaps, there would be no other guests, changing the mood of relaxation. Sure enough, Lucy prattled away until dinner was served, touching on the affairs of the children (he still didn't know their ages, or how many of them there were), about how happily Camilla wrote from New England, where she had returned with her husband, Ralph Kilmer, shortly after their marriage. Antony ventured a question there . . . had Ricky Barnard gone with them? Lucy said, 'Yes, of course,' rather as though it was something he should have known, and then went on to elaborate. 'He's twenty now, time goes so quickly, and has his application in for M.I.T., whatever that is.'

'Massachussets Institute of Technology,' said Peter. He sounded a little, a very little, over-patient, as though he had made the explanation too many times before.

'That's good. That's what he always wanted,' Maitland

told them. 'I remember him telling me that the first time I saw him, in the garden of his grandfather's house. Only at that time there didn't seem much hope of his ever getting there.'

'He writes sometimes,' said Lucy. 'I think he's happy too, but it's more difficult to tell.'

'Nonsense, of course he's happy. He's got everything he ever wanted,' said Peter, but now he was more amused than exasperated. 'As Antony says, it's exactly – '

'Oh, but, Peter, at first – '

'At first he found his new friends rather immature, but that was the fault of old Thomas's training and he soon got over it.'

'Aunt Edwina died, you know, two years ago,' said Lucy in her comfortable voice. 'And Uncle Thomas really isn't at all well. I don't think either of them ever got over . . . all that.'

'I'm sorry to hear it.' It was impossible to tell from Lucy's tone how much this was a matter of concern to her. 'While we're talking about the past,' he went on, 'what about Audrey . . . Mrs. Hill?'

Peter laughed. 'She isn't Mrs. Hill any longer,' he said. 'In fact, she's on her second husband since you saw her.' Lucy gave him a reproachful look.

'She was more upset than anybody about . . . about Alan,' she said. Antony thought that, perhaps, she was being rather determinedly charitable. 'It was quite a year before she married Carlos, and I knew that was a mistake from the beginning. But she seems quite happy now.'

'While it lasts,' said Peter, and got up to refill his wife's glass. He, no less than their guest, was taking his time over his first glass of sherry.

So the conversation continued innocuously until after dinner when they were sitting with their coffee, and Peter had produced a fine selection of liqueurs; which again Antony thought had been selected by his hostess, as they varied only a little in their degree of sweetness. He was enjoying the evening, didn't want to do anything to disturb its peaceful quality, but still he was curious. 'How long has Inspector Brady been engaged to Miss Pershing?' he asked idly, but somehow under the appearance of casualness he felt that the question was important.

Peter started to say, 'It must be of quite a recent date,' but he was interrupted by Lucy who sat up suddenly quite straight (an unwonted display of energy) and said in a surprised tone,

'Philip engaged! Nobody told me that.'

'I didn't know myself until today,' said Peter, his voice faintly apologetic to meet the reproach in hers. 'So I can't tell you anything about her, Antony. I'd never met the lady before.'

'Well, at least you can tell me something about her,' said Lucy. 'What's she like?'

'Very attractive. Red hair and a good figure,' said Peter.

'I meant – '

'Yes, I know you did, but we only saw her for a moment. I really can't give you an estimate of her character on such short acquaintance.'

That was Peter, not liking her questioning overmuch; Antony was less cautious. 'She's extremely self-possessed, for one thing,' he said. 'And she has her own brand of humour, which perhaps may not be altogether kind.'

'I thought you didn't take to her,' said Peter, somehow succeeding in making the words a question.

No need to explain that he hadn't relished the reminder of the publicity that had attended some of his cases. 'I wasn't too polite to her myself, so I suppose I shouldn't complain,' Maitland said. 'It was a surprise to you then . . . this engagement?'

'A complete and utter surprise,' said Lucy emphatically. 'All the more so because I've always thought Philip was a confirmed bachelor. I don't mean he hasn't always . . . well – '

'Flitted from flower to flower,' suggested Peter, when she seemed in some doubt as to how to continue. He was smiling, but Lucy accepted the remark in all seriousness.

'He always said there was safety in numbers.' She sounded a little worried now. 'And now you're saying this girl . . . what is her name, anyway?'

'Moira Pershing.'

'Well, you're saying she isn't very likeable.'

'If Philip likes her, that's all that matters, isn't it?'

'No, I don't think so. But at least you have to admit,' said Lucy, cheering up, 'she must be very fond of him to say she'll marry him at a time like this.'

'That's the usual basis for an engagement,' said Peter, rather shortly.

'Yes, of course. I hope, between the two of you, you managed to cheer him up when you saw him this afternoon.' She was looking at Antony as she spoke, and it was he who answered her, rather unwillingly.

'No, I can't say we did.'

'I hoped –'

'That's just the trouble. There isn't really any basis for hope, and it wouldn't be fair to make promises we couldn't begin to fulfil.' She didn't say anything to that, just sat looking stricken, and after a moment he went on. 'If you want to help – if you don't mind my turning a pleasant social occasion into a discussion of shop – you tell me something about some of the characters in this drama.'

'Anything, of course, but we don't know any of them well except Philip, and Peter says you spent quite a time together this afternoon.'

'So we did. Now, you say you'd neither of you met Miss Pershing before, but had you heard of her?'

'No,' said Lucy, but 'Not exactly,' said Peter. Maitland smiled at him.

'You'd better explain, don't you think?' he said.

'Well, I met Philip one day, about two weeks ago, and he seemed particularly depressed. So I asked him to dinner, thought it might cheer him up, but he said he couldn't make it. And then he explained, as though he couldn't help himself,

41

that there was this smashing redhead he'd met the night before. I should think that was Moira, wouldn't you?'

'It seems probable. Did he say where he'd met her?'

'In a pub. The Coach and Horses, on Water Street.'

'But still he was depressed?'

'That's right. Look here, I don't quite see why you're so interested in the wretched girl.'

'I am interested in anything that pertains to our client,' said Antony, with a touch of smugness that made Gibson smile in sympathy. 'But if you don't like the subject we'll try another one. Tell me about the plaintiffs.'

'I wasn't concerned in the original action, you know.'

'I realise that. But still, you've read the papers, and you must have got some impression of them from talking to Brady.'

'I'll do my best for you.' He was obviously going to take his time, but Maitland had no desire to hurry him. 'Dobell is a quiet type, subscribes to the symphony, haunts the local branch of W. H. Smith's, likes an occasional weekend in London to do a show.'

'For a chap who peddles cheese – '

'Yes, well, I don't know that his heart's in his work.'

'This business of investing in diamonds doesn't sound too improbable on the face of it. The thing is, where did he get the money from if he came by it honestly?'

'From his savings, he says,' said Peter doubtfully.

'So the question is, how much does he earn? Did Wellesley ask him that in the first trial?'

'I don't remember that he did. The whole thing was sprung on him, you know, so unexpectedly that you can't blame him much, even for overlooking the obvious. But I shouldn't think – I'm guessing now, Antony – that old Hargreaves is a particularly generous employer.'

'It all depends, I suppose, what the profits in the cheese business are like. Does Dobell's wife share his tastes?'

'I don't really know. He's a Mason, so there are times he leaves her to amuse herself, but I gather he doesn't mind spending money on her. I'm going by what Philip told me, of course. He says they hated each other. But there's no gossip in the town about them.' The emphasis on the last word was very faint, but Maitland pounced immediately.

'The Irvings then. Are you telling me – ?'

'Don't go so fast. It's just that I've heard when he works late she has no difficulty in amusing herself, but I've also heard that he's devoted to her.'

'I see.' He waited a moment, and then said with the first sign of impatience he had shown, 'Well, what are they like, the Irvings? John and – ?'

'Doris. I don't really know – '

'Do they share the Dobells' tastes?'

'I shouldn't think so. Philip did tell me Irving was at a soccer match when they searched the house . . . Mrs. Irving was at home, of course.'

'Any signs that they live above their income . . . their probable income, I should say? I don't suppose we know what he earns either.'

'I'm afraid not. Their main amusement seems to be going down to the pub for a drink, and meeting their friends there. But they do take a holiday on the continent most years; I don't see why that shouldn't be well within their means. As for their tastes, I only know Philip said there wasn't a book or record in the house, only the telly and a transistor radio in the kitchen.'

'Come now, that's the best news I've heard all day.'

'How do you make that out?'

'Two things. We'll assume that Irving likes to keep an eye on his wife, why then did he go to the Red Lion without her? I presume nobody claims she was there.'

'Not that I heard. And the other point?'

'Why should two men of such dissimilar tastes get together, not once, but several times?'

'Noyes now claims he never saw them together.'

'So he does. And the first point isn't much good without the other, because I don't see the judge allowing me to insinuate that Mrs. Irving is flighty, which I should have to do in order to get it over to the jury.' He turned and looked at Lucy. 'It looks as though we hadn't too much hope to offer your friend Philip after all.'

'I wish – ' said Lucy, and broke off there and looked from one of them to the other. 'It just seems so unfair. People have been found Not Guilty before, without taking action against the police.'

'That's a good point, and one we touched on in our discussion this afternoon,' Antony told her. He couldn't very well call her 'Mrs. Gibson' now that he seemed to have proceeded to Christian name terms with her husband, but somehow the informality of 'Lucy', for all her friendliness, didn't come naturally. 'We think it may be to discourage the police from making any further enquiries, in case they manage to get one step nearer the top than Dobell and Irving, you see.'

'Nearer the top?' said Lucy wonderingly.

'There's an organisation involved, at least we think there is, and they're only on the fringe of it,' Peter explained. But he didn't seem inclined to go into the matter more fully, and looked relieved when Antony took up his questioning.

'Still on the subject of the plaintiffs, do you know of any common friends?'

'No, I don't. I told you I don't know much about either of them. They both know the people at the firm, I suppose – '

'At a guess I wouldn't say we should look for the next level at Hargreaves & Company.'

'Too obvious?'

'Not exactly. It's just a feeling, that the firm wouldn't have been used if that had been the case.'

'Well, I suppose, if you get right down to it, they both knew Noyes.'

'Who is Noyes?' asked Lucy.

'The barman at the Red Lion.'

'He can't be their contact,' said Antony. 'Not if Brady's telling the truth.'

44

'Of course he is.' Lucy was inclined to be indignant. Maitland smiled at her, but did not on that occasion allow himself to be diverted from his point.

'What I was going to say was that, accepting Brady's story, Noyes told the truth at first. It was only later that he was, presumably, got at.'

'I don't know of anybody else,' said Peter. 'But there may be a dozen people living in Northdean, for all I know, with whom both of them are acquainted.'

'That's something we shall have to try to find out. Meanwhile – this is something you should be able to tell me, Peter – the two police officers who held keys to the filing cabinets in which the statements were lodged – '

'I know them both casually,' Peter admitted. 'Superintendent Harley has been in Northdean most of his working life, I think. A very well respected man.'

'Yes, I'm sure. But do you know anything about him that might interest me?'

'If you mean, is it likely that he used his key to remove the statements from the police files, I should say it's just about as unlikely as that – well, as that Philip himself took them and sabotaged his own case.'

'You think highly of him then?'

'Very highly. If I must go into details,' said Peter, obviously bored with the subject, 'I should say he's a man not without compassion. But an efficient man, on top of his job.'

'I see. No sudden signs of affluence, then?'

'His wife has money.' That was Lucy's contribution but she looked a little uneasy about it. 'I can't see why you're asking all these questions,' she complained. 'The Harleys are nice people.'

'Peter will explain it to you . . . later,' said Antony unfairly. 'It's getting late, and I ought to be going. But before I do, tell me about Sergeant Cummings, in whose nominal charge the filing cabinets were.'

'There's nothing to tell you. He's been here about three years, a good steady type, but not likely to go much beyond his present rank, I imagine. And he lives just as you would expect . . . quietly. And doesn't show any signs of having had more money than usual to spend these last weeks.'

'Thank you.' He got up as he spoke. 'One more thing . . . and you won't like it, Peter, but it's got to be asked. Do *you* believe Brady's story?'

'Of course I do.' Peter was on his feet too. 'There's so much to back it up . . . the statements disappearing . . . the fact that he brought the case at all, which he wouldn't have done if he meant to sabotage it later.'

'I have to point out that he might have had no option. Constable Peach knew as much of the evidence as he did.'

'And then he arranged with – with higher authority to have the witnesses suborned? That's theoretically possible, I grant you. But in that case, why should Dobell and Irving bring suit against him?'

'We agreed we were only guessing about why the charge was made.'

'So we did.' He broke off there, and then added with a worried look, 'For some reason you don't believe me when I say that I have implicit faith in Philip.'

'Perhaps because I think you're a little too anxious to point out the things in his favour.'

'But that's only because you don't know him as we do. Naturally I want to convince you.' He was speaking a little wildly, but then his look became intent. 'Have I?' he asked.

'Strangely enough, I don't need convincing.'

'I'm so glad!' said Lucy. Like her husband, she wore a worried look, she was also obviously bewildered, but this was something she could understand.

'It isn't what I think that matters,' Antony warned her. 'I'm sorry, Lucy,' – this time her name came quite naturally to his lips – 'to repay your kindness by badgering you both with questions. My excuse must be that I'm concerned, too.'

It was an odd thing, he considered, as he walked down the street a few minutes later, that both the Gibsons seemed

46

almost pathetically grateful for his assurances of belief in their friend.

IV

He had quite a long telephone conversation with Jenny after he got back to the hotel, but though he was half expecting it to ring again while he prepared for bed, the phone remained silent. He read for a little while and then slept well, without dreaming.

TUESDAY, 25th MAY

I

He got himself up in a leisurely fashion next morning, and found the dining-room almost empty when he went downstairs. This was to his taste, he had things to think over . . . how he was going to approach Superintendent Harley and Sergeant Cummings, for instance, without putting their backs up irrevocably. The *Northdean Daily Record* lay unheeded beside his plate.

He had just finished his second cup of coffee, and with it reached the conclusion that there was nothing for it but to go round to the police station and trust to the inspiration of the moment, when he was summoned to the telephone. 'You can take it in the box in the hall, sir,' the waiter added obligingly. Antony thanked him and went out.

He knew that phone booth of old, it was dark, and stuffy, and induced in him a distinct feeling of claustrophobia. He left the door open, and picked up the receiver with the hope that it was Peter Gibson with some good ideas as to how he should proceed.

True enough, it was Gibson, but his tone was hardly reassuring. It was, in fact, more like a bark. 'Have you seen the paper?' he demanded, interrupting Maitland's greeting.

'I haven't read it, if that's what you mean,' Maitland replied with rather maddening precision.

'You might have missed it anyway.' Peter was making an obvious effort to speak calmly. 'It's a Stop Press item on the back page. I'll read it to you.' There was the briefest of intervals – just time for him to fold the paper to his liking, Antony thought – before he went on. ' "Clifford Dobell, 51, of 3 Marshlands Crescent, Northdean, was found dead last

48

night by his wife, Stephanie. It is understood that the police have been called in." '

'Clifford . . . that's our Dobell, isn't it?'

'Of course it is! You see what this means, don't you, Antony?'

'It means the case against Philip Brady is as dead as mutton. Unless Irving wants to begin again from the beginning, of course.'

'I know that.' Gibson was impatient. 'I meant the bit about the police being called in.'

'Don't jump to conclusions, Peter. For one thing, the reporter may have got it wrong, that's not unknown. For another, it may just be that Dobell hadn't had occasion to see his doctor lately.'

'It could mean that,' agreed Gibson grudgingly. 'But it's much more likely to mean they suspect foul play.'

It wasn't often Antony was in the position of counselling another man against incautious guesswork. 'I wonder why you're so ready to jump to that conclusion,' he said.

'Because . . . oh, because its too damn convenient,' said Peter, the exasperation in his voice very marked now. 'It was you who persuaded me there was an organisation involved in the diamond smuggling, and now you're trying to tell me – '

'I'm not trying to tell you anything. What exactly are you afraid of, Peter?'

'I think I'd better come round and see you,' said Gibson abruptly, and rang off. Maitland went back to the dining-room and his third cup of coffee.

When the solicitor arrived they went up to Antony's room. The bed had been made, and somehow the small chaos he had left behind him had been reduced to order. There was a chintz-covered armchair by the window and Gibson took that, while Maitland perched himself on the dressing-table stool. 'The ball's in your court, Peter,' he said.

Gibson hesitated. 'We agreed we weren't sure why the action was being brought,' he said at last, 'but whatever way

49

you look at it it seems that somebody's out for blood as far as Philip's concerned. Mightn't this be another move in the game?'

'You mean, first that you suspect murder, and secondly that some evidence is likely to be found pointing to Brady's guilt. Killing Dobell seems rather drastic for that purpose, don't you think? Presumably he was a member of the organisation in good standing.'

'It sounds ridiculous, I know, and I wouldn't be thinking it if it weren't for the fact that you're here.'

'Come now, what difference can that possibly make?'

'If it was suspected that Dobell couldn't stand up to the kind of enquiries *you* would instigate – ' He left the sentence there, but he had said enough.

Maitland said slowly, 'I don't much like the sound of that. It would mean . . . well, that I'm becoming a sort of jinx, wouldn't it?'

'Nothing so bad as that – '

'There's this much in favour of your idea,' said Antony, ignoring him, ' "they" certainly know I'm here.'

'How do you know?'

'There was a phone call on Sunday night after I spoke to you. No words spoken, except by me. Mr. X – I feel almost as badly as Uncle Nick does about calling him that – has played that trick before.'

'Then – '

'Look here, Peter, for all we know the man died of a heart attack.'

'Well, I'm jolly well going to find out.'

'How?'

'By going round to the police station.'

'If you'll forgive me, I don't think that's wise. If you're wrong it will leave you feeling foolish; while if you're right – '

'If I'm right – ' prompted Gibson eagerly when his companion paused.

'If you're right it would only put ideas in someone's head.'

'I don't understand.'

'You've realised, of course, that if Dobell has been murdered your friend, Philip, is the obvious suspect. Even without the sort of frame-up you seem to be postulating,' he added bluntly, cutting across Peter's protest. 'He saw his lawyers yesterday, and I don't suppose our talk left him feeling very optimistic about the outcome of the trial, do you? And he knows as well as we do that an action dies with the death of one of the parties.'

'Let me understand you, Antony. Are you saying you think *Philip* is guilty?'

'Heaven and earth! We don't even know a crime has been committed yet. But if Dobell has been murdered . . . you said yourself it's too convenient.'

Before Gibson could reply to that the telephone rang. Antony got up to answer it, glad of the release of movement. 'There's Inspector Brady to see you, Mr. Maitland,' said the desk clerk apologetically. 'I told him you had someone with you, but – '

'Thank you. Send him up,' said Antony, and went to set the bedroom door hospitably open.

Philip Brady came in tempestuously; Antony was reminded of a cat with its fur ruffled. 'The office said I'd find you here, Peter, and I'm glad of it.' His speech had quickened, so that his words were almost blurred. 'I think I need you both,' he said.

Maitland was closing the door. He did it rather slowly and carefully, well enough aware that Gibson, who was also on his feet, had flashed him a glance of triumph. Still with his hand on the knob he said, 'Sit down then, and tell us about it,' and hoped that his tone would have a dampening effect on the newcomer's excitement.

'You haven't heard what's happened!'

'If you mean Dobell's death, it was in the Stop Press,' said Peter. He too was speaking slowly and carefully, obviously with an eye to his friend's reactions.

'Was it? That was quick work.' For some reason, the

51

information seemed to have had a calming effect, so that Brady spoke in something much nearer his normal manner.

Antony took the opportunity to say again, 'Sit down, both of you.' He was conscious of a stirring of excitement himself (excitement, or foreboding?) and consciously suppressed the emotion. If Peter by any chance was right there'd better be some calm discussion of the matter. With this in mind he seated himself at the end of the bed, though he would much rather have remained standing and free to prowl about the room. After a moment's hesitation Brady took the stool and Peter sat down again. 'Does your news concern Dobell's death?' asked Antony; which he felt was an obtuse question, but one that had to be asked.

'Dobell's death!' said Brady and laughed, but not as though he were amused. 'He was murdered, didn't the paper tell you that?'

'No,' Peter told him. 'It just said the police had been called in. That would mean you, wouldn't it?'

'It should do. Not this time though. The station sergeant recognised Dobell's name, of course . . . the case has been the main topic of conversation for weeks now. So he got straight on to the Superintendent, and he decided they could do very well without me, in the circumstances.'

'Don't you think it's just as well?' Gibson was too obviously trying to exercise a calming influence. He glanced at Maitland as he spoke, rather as though daring him to be indiscreet enough to bring up the subject of their recent conversation.

'I might,' said Brady, and laughed again rather wildly, 'if it didn't mean he'd got it into his head that I had a better motive than anyone else for wanting Dobell dead.'

It was time to take a hand. Antony said, his manner as casual as he could make it, 'How did he die?'

'He was stabbed,' said Brady. His voice held a rather savage satisfaction, rather as if he wished he had held the knife himself. Or as though the memory of what he had done gave him pleasure? It was impossible to be sure. Maitland said, a little sharply,

'It would be as well if you gave us as many details as you can.'

'Yes, of course,' said Brady more soberly. 'The trouble is, I don't know much. His wife found him dead at ten thirty . . . and I only know that because Harley had the gall to ask me for an alibi for that time.'

'Were you able to satisfy him?'

'I was with Moira, *that*'s all right.'

Maitland said nothing to that; his eyes had a puzzled look. Peter, sounding rather like a teacher encouraging a backward pupil, said bracingly, 'I can't see why you should think you need our services then.'

'Not as lawyer and client.' He seemed to find the explanation distasteful. 'But you're a friend of mine, Peter, and I thought,' – he turned his head to look at Antony – 'I thought . . . yesterday . . . that you seemed inclined to be friendly too.'

'Certainly.' There was more warmth in Maitland's smile than he perhaps intended. 'You want our advice,' he hazarded.

'I don't know what to do. I've always thought . . . I like my job, I'm not much given to introspection, everything seemed pretty straightforward.'

'And now that's all changed,' agreed Antony sympathetically. But Peter said, almost at the same moment,

'I don't see the difficulty, I'm afraid.'

'Don't you? What would you do, Peter, if old What's-his-name – your senior partner – practically accused you of committing murder?'

'If I could prove, as you say you can, that I was somewhere else at the time – '

'That's not the point,' said Brady stubbornly.

'If I were you I'd accept his apology and forget the whole thing,' said Maitland, when Gibson made no attempt to complete his sentence.

'But he hasn't apologised!'

'I expect he will when he's checked with Miss Pershing.'

53

'Well . . . perhaps.'

'Take your time to think about it before rushing in with your resignation at least.'

Brady turned his head, to catch Peter's eye. 'Is that your advice too?' he asked.

'It is. After all, Philip, even if you feel you can never work with Harley again, you can ask for a transfer when all this has blown over.'

'I suppose you're right.' He still sounded reluctant. Maitland said, before Brady could speak again,

'What were your relations with Superintendent Harley before today?'

'Good, I suppose. I never thought about it.'

'How would you describe him?' said Antony, thinking of his conversation with the Gibsons the previous night.

'A decent enough sort of chap. That's why it hit me so hard, I expect. I mean, why should he think such a thing, without any evidence?'

Peter opened his mouth to speak, and then closed it again. This time it was Maitland who sent a warning look in his colleague's direction. 'I'd go back to work, if I were you,' he advised. 'But – a word of warning – I shouldn't try to get in touch with Miss Pershing until the Superintendent has spoken to her. He might suspect collusion.'

Brady got to his feet. 'I won't go near her,' he promised bitterly. 'But it shows you what things have come to, doesn't it. Collusion!' he added, as if it were an imprecation, and made for the door.

When they were left alone together Maitland looked at Gibson and smiled. 'That solves your problem, doesn't it?' he said. 'You know, you almost had me believing in some deep, dark plot to involve our friend.'

'And now it seems he's in the clear,' said Peter, relieved.

'Just rather angry, and he'll get over that,' Antony agreed. 'Now I'd better be thinking of getting back to town.'

For some reason Gibson seemed to find this idea a little daunting. 'Oh . . . must you?' he said.

'Can you think of any reason why not? If Irving does decide to go ahead on his own I can come back again when the time comes. Meanwhile, there's nothing for me to do.'

'I don't know . . . I'm uneasy.' He paused there, and then added with a smile that didn't quite come off, 'Don't take any notice of me, Antony. I've scared myself with a bogeyman that doesn't exist, or you've scared me with all this talk about Mr. X. But, as you say, that's no concern of ours unless and until Irving takes some action.' He hesitated again, and then said, rather as though he found the words difficult, 'The best train is the afternoon one, five past four as far as I remember.'

'In that case I'll see if Vera's free, and if she is take the bus over to Chedcombe and have lunch with her. Tell Lucy how much I enjoyed myself yesterday evening, and apologise again for our talking shop. If we'd known we needn't have bored her with it.'

'You'll explain the position to Miss Langhorne then, either on the telephone or in person,' said Peter, making for the door. 'You know, you'll think I'm psychic or something, but I have the strangest feeling we haven't heard the last of all this yet.'

In the event he proved to be a true prophet. Antony, descending from the Chedcombe bus in the square and strolling leisurely towards the hotel to retrieve his suitcase, found Peter Gibson waiting for him on the doorstep. 'I've re-booked your room for you and got them to take your case back upstairs,' he said without preamble.

Antony reached his side. 'Something's happened,' he said.

'You can say that again,' Peter told him grimly. 'Philip has been arrested for Dobell's murder.'

II

Maitland made no comment on that until they were upstairs in his room – the same room he had vacated that morning – with the door firmly shut. Then he said, a statement rather than a question, 'His alibi didn't hold up.'

'That's only part of it.'

'Take a deep breath and start at the beginning,' Antony advised. Peter gave him a rather abstracted smile.

'Philip phoned home to tell me what had happened while I was still at lunch,' he said. 'I couldn't understand it, after what he told us this morning, but of course I told him to keep his mouth shut and I'd be with him right away. When I got to the station I had a talk with Philip, and then with Superintendent Harley, but it will make more sense if I give it to you the other way around. The police case is . . . well, first of all there's Mrs. Dobell's evidence. She says they were at home that evening, listening to a symphony concert on the radio. Just the two of them, there's a son but he works over in Chedcombe and is in lodgings there. When the programme was over Mrs. Dobell – her name is Stephanie – went up to bed, but Dobell said he would stay up and finish his book. At ten thirty-five she heard the front door close and footsteps going down the path to the gate.'

'It's a little odd – don't you think? – that she should be so accurate about the time.'

'Not really. She was reading, so the light was on, and she glanced at the bedside clock. She hadn't heard anybody arrive, so her first idea was that it must be her husband going out, and that made her curious because he wasn't in the habit of taking a constitutional before retiring, so she got up and went to the window. She recognised Philip, who was just going through the front gate.'

'She only saw his back then?'

'No, he turned to make sure the latch had caught. I asked about fingerprints, of course, but there weren't any, only smudges. Stephanie Dobell says she knows Philip quite well by sight, she saw him on several occasions when the case against Dobell was being prepared.'

'What did she do then?'

56

'She said she had a feeling something was wrong. She went downstairs and found her husband dead.'

'Stabbed, Brady said.'

'I'm coming to that in a minute, but certainly he was stabbed.'

'That was the point, I suppose, at which Harley interviewed Brady, without saying anything about the identification.'

'That's right. He went straight out to verify the alibi, and Miss Pershing told him she'd been out to dinner with Philip and he went back to her flat with her, but left her at ten o'clock saying he had a report to write before turning in.'

'What are the respective positions of Miss Pershing's apartment and Dobell's house?'

'He could have walked the distance easily in a quarter of an hour.'

'I see. And what has Brady to say to that?'

'Everything was as she said except the time he left her. He says it was twelve thirty, and nothing at all was said about writing a report.'

'At which point Superintendent Harley, not unnaturally, made up his mind –'

'I think he did. He warned Philip and asked him again about the alibi, but Philip stuck to his story. Then Harley showed him the knife that had been used, that was still sticking out of Dobell's chest when his wife found him. And Philip had no more sense than to blurt out, "but that's mine". After which, of course, all hell broke loose.'

'You mean, Brady was arrested.'

'Yes.' Peter smiled again, wryly. 'Only, you see, I can't think about it quite as calmly as you can.'

'I appreciate that. Were his fingerprints found inside the house?'

'No. But Philip, of all people, would have known enough to wear gloves.'

'That argument would go a fair way towards proving

premeditation, if the ownership of the knife wasn't enough on its own.'

'That wasn't my intention.'

'I don't suppose it was. Had Superintendent Harley anything else to tell you?'

'Don't you think that was enough?'

'To be going on with,' Maitland agreed. 'You haven't told me yet what Brady had to say.'

'About his alibi – '

'Yes, he says he was with Miss Pershing until after midnight. I hadn't forgotten. When was the arrangement made that they should spend the evening together?'

'I'm afraid I can't tell you that.'

'What did he have to say about Mrs. Dobell's statement then?'

'Only that she must have been mistaken.'

'And about the knife?'

'He admitted it was his. What else could there be to say about it?'

'A good deal, I should have thought.' Antony got up and stood looking down at his companion. 'It seems your first idea was right, Peter.'

'I said I didn't think we'd heard the end of it.'

'Go back to first thing this morning, before Brady came to see us. You thought there might be a conspiracy to involve him.'

'Well, I did think so, but in view of what has happened – ' Again he broke off what he was saying, and looked rather helplessly at Maitland.

Antony took a quick turn to the bathroom door and back again. 'Say what you mean,' he urged, when he once more came to a halt.

'If you can't see – ' Gibson seemed incapable of completing a sentence. Antony answered without waiting for him to finish.

'I can see there's something in the evidence that disturbs you.'

'Disturbs me! The whole thing disturbs me!'

'Something in particular,' Maitland insisted.

'There's the fact that he owns the murder weapon, for one thing. And then Moira Pershing's evidence. She's engaged to him, Antony. She wouldn't have given him the lie if she could have helped it.'

'So you think he's guilty.' Maitland sounded thoughtful. 'That's odd, you know, because this morning I thought you were being fanciful, but now it seems to me that you were in the right of it.' He paused there, as though waiting for some comment, but when none was forthcoming went on. 'Just why, in the circumstances, did you want me to stay?'

'Only until tomorrow. There's the Magistrates' Court hearing at eleven, but before that I thought we could see Philip together, perhaps he'd admit to you where he won't to me –'

'You mean to act for him then?'

'Of course. He's a friend, nothing alters that, I'll do my best for him. What I thought – I don't seem to be explaining myself very well – is that you might be able to persuade him to tell us the truth, then we could decide how best to deal with the defence.'

'But my estimate of the truth and yours don't seem to have much in common.'

'I know, and I don't understand it.'

'Two points, Peter. Would Brady have been surprised when he saw the knife – so surprised that he admitted its ownership – if he knew damn well he'd stabbed Dobell with it himself? Would he have been so careless as to allow himself to be seen by Mrs. Dobell? If her story is true, we must presume he shut the front door and walked down the path with no special precautions against being heard, and then turned and carefully shut the gate behind him. And above all, would he have put forward an alibi that he knew could be so easily disproved?'

'That's three points, not two,' Gibson objected. 'And I think the answer is that he was shocked by what he had done and that was how he came to make mistakes. Moira Pershing would never have lied – '

'Don't you think so?'

Something in his tone brought Peter up short. 'I know you didn't like the lady, but isn't that carrying prejudice a little too far?'

'Well, for one thing, she wasn't – isn't – in love with Brady.'

'How do you make that out?'

'I came to Northdean in his interests . . . remember? She would never have tried to antagonise me if she really cared what happened to him.'

'I wish I believed you, Antony, but I don't.'

'Then we must agree to differ. What do you want me to do?'

'See Philip tomorrow, attend the Magistrates' Court hearing. I don't suppose the case itself will come on until autumn.'

'I won't accept a brief from you, if that's what you mean.'

For a moment Gibson stared at him. 'Because you don't agree with me,' he began at last slowly, but Maitland didn't allow him to finish.

'In a way that's true,' he said. 'Because I don't agree with you I want to be free to investigate the case myself. And I don't mean next month, or during the autumn assize, Peter, I mean here and now.'

'But – '

'If you're worried about the hearing tomorrow, why don't you ask Uncle Nick to come here?'

'Would he?'

'We can but try.' He stopped, looked at Peter questioningly for a moment, and then laughed. 'All right, it's my idea, I'll telephone him myself since the matter is urgent. But you'll have to talk to Mallory.'

'Mallory?' said Gibson. He seemed to be stunned by the sudden decisiveness of Maitland's manner.

'My uncle's clerk. We'll be disrupting his carefully planned schedule and he won't be pleased with us, but he's less likely to say so to you than to me.'

III

It was not to be expected that Sir Nicholas would take the request calmly, but when Antony was in mid-flight with his explanations his uncle reversed course suddenly and became almost amiable. 'Of course it would be no trouble to cancel my engagements and catch the late train at such short notice,' he said dulcetly. 'It does occur to me to wonder, however, why you think my presence necessary at what is no more than a formal hearing.'

'I'm needed in the background, Uncle Nick. It will be better if I don't appear myself.'

'That I understand. But surely in the circumstances your friend, Gibson – '

'He'd do his best, I know. Brady is a friend of his. The trouble is though, he doesn't believe a word he says about last night.'

'You are hoping I shall prove more . . . credulous?' said Sir Nicholas, but went on without waiting for his nephew to reply. 'Well, I will come, and I too will do my best, but on one condition.'

'What is that?' asked Maitland warily.

'That you prevail upon Miss Langhorne to attend the hearing too.'

'But, Uncle Nick – ' He was relieved that the stipulation did not concern his own activities, but perhaps even more astonished.

'I cannot possibly act without a junior,' said Sir Nicholas blandly. 'Besides, she will have been holding herself in readiness to come to Northdean in connection with the wrongful arrest case.'

'I only told her at lunch time – ' But he thought he saw now; it was a simple act of kindness, which of course his uncle would never admit. Vera Langhorne, as he was very well aware, didn't have the most remunerative practice in the world.

'Then you had better ring off now and explain the changed position to her without any more delay. That will have the added advantage,' said Nicholas, suddenly tart again, 'of allowing me to make the necessary preparations for this very unexpected journey.'

IV

It wasn't difficult to persuade Vera; she promised to catch the early bus next morning, and Antony was able to report success when he met his uncle at the station that evening. Sir Nicholas was a little ruffled from his journey, and from the necessity of eating his dinner on the train, but he condescended to join the bar mess – now almost at full strength – for a glass of cognac, and went to bed eventually in an almost mellow frame of mind. Though he did not forget to say, as he parted from his nephew in the corridor outside his room, 'We will talk in the morning, Antony.'

There was a faintly ominous ring to that, but on the whole Maitland went to his room well contented.

WEDNESDAY, 26th MAY

I

If Sir Nicholas had been intending to complain further about his involvement in the case, he was to some extent frustrated by the fact that Vera Langhorne turned up, true to her promise, at a few minutes to eight o'clock. He was already in the dining-room when she came into the hotel, but Antony was in the hall. He was pleased to see her, and said so. 'Come and have some breakfast with us.'

'Already eaten. Cup of coffee,' said Vera, a little out of breath.

'I can't tell you how glad I am to see you,' he said again, and added, in response to her enquiring look, 'Uncle Nick isn't best pleased to be dragged away from town. You can help me draw his fire.'

She didn't reply to that except with her rather grim smile, which he knew from experience denoted a genuine amusement. 'There's quite a lot to tell you,' he said, taking her arm and urging her towards the dining-room. She was wearing one of her usual sack-like garments with a light raincoat thrown on over it, and her thick hair was not altogether tidy, but she was one of his favourite people and he was glad his uncle had thought to include her in their council of war.

Sir Nicholas was smiling when he got up to greet the newcomer. 'My dear Miss Langhorne,' he said, 'it was good of you to respond to our appeal so promptly.'

'Only too glad.' Vera threw herself down in the chair Antony was holding for her. 'Besides . . . curious,' she admitted, and smiled from one of them to the other.

'I have to agree,' said Sir Nicholas, seating himself again in his more leisurely way, 'that my nephew's explanations

63

over the telephone left something to be desired. However, he will no doubt remedy the matter while we eat. They can offer us kippers, if that is to your taste.'

'Thank you, just some coffee,' said Vera, and was left to catch her breath while the waiter was given his instructions.

When the man had gone Sir Nicholas leaned back in his chair. 'And now, my dear boy,' he said. It occurred to Antony to wonder whether Miss Langhorne was at all deceived by the urbanity of his tone. 'We await what I am sure will prove to be an illuminating discourse.'

There was nothing for it but to start all over from the beginning; he was conscious enough of the sketchy nature of the outline he had given his uncle before. Vera listened in silence, sipping her coffee, her eyes fixed on his face. Rather unnervingly, Sir Nicholas refrained from comment too, devoting himself to his breakfast when it arrived with a placidity that might have argued inattention, but Antony knew better than that. When he had finished speaking his kipper was cold, but he had managed to drink one cup of coffee and there was still a good, hot, strong brew in the pot. As he was pouring it Sir Nicholas put down his knife and fork with a rather exaggerated care and said, addressing himself to a point somewhere between his companions, 'So Gibson's first thought on hearing of Dobell's death was the rather melodramatic one that somehow your Mr. X must be involved.'

'That's right.'

'If I understand you correctly, you did not at that juncture subscribe to that idea.'

'That's right too. It seemed to me to be just what you've called it . . . melodramatic.'

'But since then – ?'

'I changed my mind. You see, I didn't think – I don't think – that Philip Brady is a murderer.'

'That seems to be rather a far out conclusion, even for you. What do you think about it, Miss Langhorne?'

'Don't like the idea of his giving a false alibi,' said Vera succinctly.

'But that's the point, don't you see?' There was no doubt that Maitland was very much in earnest, and his uncle permitted himself a look of vague surprise. 'I think he was telling the truth about that too.'

'And is being framed?' Sir Nicholas was sceptical. 'Even Gibson, who is a friend of his you say, doesn't believe that in the face of the evidence.'

'That's why I needed your help, Uncle Nick. An enquiry must be made if we're to prevent the most frightful miscarriage of justice.'

'Perhaps. But by you?'

'Who else? From all I hear, the police are satisfied they've got their man.'

'I should like to point out two things to you, Antony. One is that you may well be wrong – '

'I don't think so.'

' – and the other is that, if you are right, you will be putting yourself deliberately in Mr. X's way.'

'I was hoping,' said Maitland, with a show of candour, 'that you wouldn't realise that.'

'I am not yet in my dotage,' said Sir Nicholas sourly. 'The matter leaps to the attention.'

'Unwise,' said Vera. 'Dangerous,' she amplified, in case either of her listeners had mistaken her drift.

'I know all that. It just seems to me something that has to be done. Think about it a minute, Uncle Nick.'

'Granting your premise – '

'Brady is innocent, I'm sure of it.'

'You will forgive me for not yet being able to agree with you.' Sir Nicholas was being manoeuvred into a position he didn't relish, and his tone accurately conveyed his displeasure.

'For the sake of argument – '

'If you insist then, Antony, I will accept your hypothesis for the sake of argument,' said Sir Nicholas, giving in suddenly. But he could not refrain from adding, on a rather acid note, 'Given your well-known love of meddling, I don't see what else you can do.'

'And you'll accept Peter's brief?'

'Mallory has already done so.'

Antony grinned at that. 'Under protest, I'll be bound.' He looked at Vera and added, encouragingly, 'If I find out who really killed Dobell – which doesn't seem likely, I admit, but I'm going to try – *if* I do you may neither of you be called upon for any action beyond today.'

'Can't see it,' said Vera, shaking her head. 'Why should the girl lie?'

'Moira Pershing seems to be worrying you more than anything else.'

'Don't like the evidence about the weapon either. Or Mrs. Dobell's story.'

For the moment, Maitland ignored that. 'All I can say is, if you'd seen them together –'

'Be a little more explicit, Antony,' his uncle adjured him. 'If we'd seen –'

'Moira Pershing and Philip Brady. She doesn't care tuppence for him, and as Peter says they only met a fortnight ago I'd say that was a put-up job too.'

'Like the other evidence,' said Sir Nicholas thoughtfully. 'Well, you know your own business best, Antony,' – his tone made it obvious that this was a downright lie – 'but the whole thing seems to me to be extremely unlikely. For instance why, according to your theory, was Dobell killed?'

Antony hesitated over that. 'I think . . . I'm afraid,' he said at last, reluctantly, 'that it may have been because it became known that I was going to defend the wrongful arrest suit.'

'A deep-laid scheme, evidently, to plant Miss Pershing here so long before the event.'

Maitland flushed a little at the older man's tone. 'I accepted the brief three weeks ago,' he said, rather doggedly. 'Things like that get known, and Mr. X must be a good organiser to be where he is today. He made sure I was here before he gave the signal for action – '

'Even so . . . why?'

'Perhaps because Dobell was the weak link in the chain, the sort of man who would come apart under the kind of pressure I'd be likely to apply. I mean, you see, if somebody had taken the case who didn't care particularly one way or the other . . . I suppose I'm saying, he thinks me more credulous than the next man,' he added, and laughed ruefully.

Sir Nicholas started to say, 'So long as you realise that – ' but stopped when Vera began to speak almost at the same moment.

'Could be true, you know. Dobell's death would do just as well to discredit Brady.'

'My dear Miss Langhorne!' Sir Nicholas sounded serious enough, but to Antony at least his eyes betrayed his amusement. 'I hoped for your co-operation in holding the line somewhere this side of sanity.'

'Been right before,' insisted Vera gruffly.

'On occasions, yes. On others – ' He shrugged. 'Some day when we are more at leisure I will entertain you with the details. At present – you will appreciate this – I should like to know how Mr. X persuaded Mrs. Dobell to contribute to Brady's undoing. She must have suspected, at least, if he approached her, that the murder was of his contriving.'

'For one thing, he wouldn't approach her in person – '

'I understand that, but the point is immaterial.'

' – and for another, I gathered from the Gibsons that the lady won't exactly be inconsolable.'

'Then tell me your theory about the knife.'

'I haven't one, until I talk to Brady.'

'When do you propose to do that?'

'This afternoon, I thought.'

'This morning – '

'You'll be busy with him yourselves before the hearing. I'd rather see him alone, so I'll talk to Wellesley first, he told me last night he'd be free.' He paused and drank the last of his coffee, looking from one of them to the other. 'I'll see you in court,' he said.

'Do they mean to elaborate their case this morning?'

'Peter thinks so. Well, that's why I wanted you here. There's no earthly reason why they shouldn't, anyway, all the evidence seems to be in.'

'I shouldn't be so sure of that, if I were you. If by any chance you're right – '

'You're making my flesh creep, Uncle Nick.'

'Am I?' enquired Sir Nicholas placidly. Antony grinned at him, but did not make any more direct reply.

'Peter recommends the afternoon train,' he said. 'I hope you'll be in time to catch it.'

'As it happens, I do not intend to return to London immediately.'

Maitland was half-way to his feet, but now he sank back in his chair again. 'But – ' he said, and stopped there because he couldn't think of any words forceful enough to convey his bewilderment.

'There is no reason that I can see why I should not take a holiday if I wish.'

'I'd forgotten about Whitsuntide.'

'So it seems. I have, however, made it clear to Mallory that I shall not necessarily return for the beginning of the Trinity term.'

'But – ' said Antony again. This time it was Vera who interrupted him.

'Pleasant time of year. Seems a good idea,' she said.

'Precisely. And as I gather you intend to be here for some time yourself, Antony, I shall ask Jenny to join us, bringing the car.'

'Good idea. See something of the countryside,' said Vera approvingly. Antony was still speechless, but he thought he saw now what was in the wind: Sir Nicholas intended to keep a watchful eye on his activities, a thing he had never done before at the beginning of a case, though there had been two occasions, still vivid in his memory, when his

68

uncle had returned in some haste from abroad. That was all very well, but it gave him something of the feeling of one who has conjured up a demon and then finds himself powerless to be rid of it.

'I'm going home myself for the weekend,' he said, finding his voice at last.

'In that case I will go up to town myself tomorrow, and return when you do. But I thought you said that Inspector Brady's problems were to take precedence over everything else.'

'I want to talk to Roger. I'll explain that later,' he added hurriedly, when Sir Nicholas bent on him an enquiring eye. 'It's just an idea I have – ' He didn't want to amplify that; he let the sentence trail into silence.

'If I know anything of your ideas, Antony – '

'Well, this is quite a harmless one. Look here, Uncle Nick – ' But what was the use of trying to have it out with him, when he was a past master in the art of evading any topic he did not wish to pursue? Maitland got to his feet.

'I don't think there's anything more to be said at the moment,' he told them, 'and I promised to see Wellesley in his room at nine.'

'In any event, it's time we made for Gibson's office,' said Sir Nicholas, getting up in his turn. 'If you are ready, Miss Langhorne?'

Vera picked up a bulging handbag. 'Any time,' she said obligingly.

II

Antony went to the door to see them off, pointed out the way to Westgate Street, and then recalled that Vera probably knew the town well enough. She accepted his directions with apparent gratitude, however, and stumped off along the side of the square at Sir Nicholas's side. Maitland watched them go, an incongruous couple, and was frowning slightly as he turned to re-enter the hotel, rather as if something puzzled him. But whatever it was, he seemed to dismiss it quickly from his mind. He shrugged his shoulders, glanced at his watch, made in some haste for the staircase.

Wellesley, who had been the prosecuting counsel when Dobell and Irving were tried for diamond smuggling, was an old friend. If he had been inclined to plumpness when first they met, some fourteen years before, he was now unashamedly rotund, but his eyes had not lost their bright, enquiring look, nor his face its appearance of innocent amiability. He had just finished breakfast when Maitland arrived, and was still in his dressing-gown. 'So you've got Sir Nicholas down,' he said by way of greeting. 'I remember you playing that game before.'

'And Vera Langhorne, they make a good team,' said Antony, declining to be drawn.

'Yes, that's all very well. Means you're going to poke about in the background if it means anything at all,' said Wellesley. 'You think there's something to be said for Brady, then . . . something that's worth investigating?'

'I think there's a good deal to be said for him. That he's innocent, for instance.'

'That isn't like you.' Wellesley was a little surprised, but much more amused. Antony felt a sudden stab of irritation. 'I've known you on a quest before,' Wellesley went on, 'and usually you're plagued by doubts.'

That brought Maitland up short. He didn't like the feeling that the workings of his mind were as an open book to the onlooker, but he had to admit the truth of the statement. 'I suppose it is odd,' he said, after he had taken a moment to consider it. 'Brady is a man I could like, I think, but that's not it. I mean, I know well enough – '

'That one's likes and dislikes have very little to do with anything. I'm sure you know that by this time, but something seems to have convinced you. It would be interesting to know what it is. Instinct, perhaps.'

Antony had a sour look for that suggestion. Instinct was

a thing he would have said he particularly distrusted. 'Let's take it as read,' he requested, 'and carry on. What can you tell me about the statements that disappeared?'

'You know, for the life of me I can't see why you want to enquire into that. The case is dead, and isn't likely to be resuscitated at this stage of the game.'

'I'm interested all right,' said Maitland a little grimly.

'That means you think there's some connection. Have the police got a case against Brady, or are they just falling over backwards not to show favouritism to one of their own men?'

'They've got a case,' Antony assured him. 'And heaven preserve me from my friends who are in the same line of business as myself. I never knew a chap so full of questions.'

Wellesley ignored the complaint. 'And yet you think he's not guilty. I don't understand it, I'm afraid,' he grumbled. 'The only connection between the two cases must surely be that the wrongful arrest action gives Brady an excellent motive for the murder.'

'On the other hand,' said Antony, rather gently because he was growing impatient, 'there is no real need for you to understand it, is there?'

Wellesley laughed. 'No need at all,' he agreed cheerfully. 'All right then, what do you want to know?'

'About the statements,' Antony reminded him.

'Yes, well, I can't tell you, of my own knowledge, that the signatures were genuine.'

'I realise that, of course. All the same – '

'I admit I never doubted their authenticity for a moment. Why should I? I don't now, for that matter. I don't think Brady would have been fool enough to go to court with no case at all. But that's a different matter to swearing.'

'I know all that.' Maitland wasn't trying to hide his impatience now. 'Be a good chap and tell me – '

'It won't be much help,' Wellesley warned him. 'The papers came into chambers in the usual way, I studied them

– also as usual – and then they were filed away.'

'Who filed them?'

'One of the junior clerks, named Bassett. He swears he put those particular documents with the others. Well, he wasn't called on to swear it, of course, I'm using the word colloquially.'

'We shall get on better if you assume that I am bringing a modicum of intelligence to bear on your answers,' Maitland assured him, and Wellesley laughed again.

'You're growing very like Sir Nicholas,' he said.

'Am I?' queried Antony blankly. It wasn't the first time the accusation had been made, but it always took him by surprise.

'Take my word for it. I should watch it if I were you.'

Maitland decided to ignore that. 'Go on then,' he urged.

'Where to?'

'Where was the filing cabinet situated? Was it locked? Who had the keys?'

Wellesley held up a protesting hand. 'Wait a bit,' he said. 'One question at a time is enough.' But he went on to answer all three without hesitation. 'The filing cabinet is in the clerks' office. From what Jameson tells it isn't kept locked during the day, only at night time. And he and I hold the only sets of keys.'

'Jameson being – ?'

'My clerk.'

'I see. Can I talk to him? And to – what's his name? – Bassett?'

'For all the good it will do you.'

'Look here, nobody's denying that – genuine or not – the statements have disappeared. Who do you think took them?'

'It's hard to believe – '

'You must have thought about this. For what it's worth I think it will prove to be the most obvious person.'

'Jameson's been with me for years.'

'Has he any particular ambitions? Travel? A house in the country? A new car?'

'I haven't the faintest idea.' For the moment Wellesley sounded just a little sulky. 'It's easier to think that one of the junior clerks . . . and of them I suppose you'd say Bassett was the most likely because he certainly knew exactly where the statements were. But even so – '

'I know! You're too nice-minded really to suspect him. Well, I may not get round to interviewing them. If things begin to move – '

'How, and in what direction?'

'I don't know.' And that was true enough. There'd be some reaction from Mr. X when he found that Maitland was still espousing Brady's cause, but what that reaction might be was another matter. Something, if the truth were told, that he didn't care to speculate about.

Wellesley had recovered his spirits. 'If the case against Brady is as strong as you implied,' he said, 'I don't see what movement is possible, except that he'll be committed for trial and in due course convicted.'

Antony got up. 'Not if I have anything to do with it,' he said, and was surprised as he spoke that he should have bothered to register his partnership so strongly. Somehow Brady's plight had got under his skin, and he wasn't even sure whether it was sympathy for the accused man or a desire to have a crack at the unknown Mr. X that motivated him more strongly. On the whole, he thought it was sympathy, and that was a poor state of mind in which to begin an investigation. So he took a quick turn about the room, while Wellesley followed his movements with a look at once enquiring and amused. 'If I don't come up with anything,' said Antony, coming to a halt again and giving his companion a rather worried look, 'we may call you and your clerks when the trial comes on.'

'I don't see what good it would do you. It would be negative evidence at best.'

'I know that. Only it would be a way – the only way open to us – of attacking the motive the prosecution will cite.'

'But you say it may not come to trial.'

'Let's hope not. And I shouldn't have said that, it's tempting providence.'

'I shouldn't worry about that,' said Wellesley dryly. 'Is that all you wanted from me?' he added, as he saw Maitland making for the door.

'If I thought there was anything more –'

'There isn't. Except my impression of Brady. I saw quite a lot of him while the case was being prepared, you know.'

Antony stopped with his hand on the door-knob. 'I should like to hear that,' he said.

'He's an intelligent chap. I said he wouldn't have been fool enough to bring that case unless he was genuinely convinced it was a good one. But he's impulsive. I can easily see the counter-action infuriating him to a point where his mood would easily explode into violence. If anything triggered him off –'

'We'd had a rather depressing talk that afternoon.'

'Then don't be too sure he didn't do it.'

'Very well.' But he knew as he spoke that was a piece of advice he wasn't going to heed. 'Thank you,' he said. 'I'm grateful.' And pulled the door open and went out into the corridor.

III

The room that was used for proceedings before the magistrates was adjacent to the police station, a good piece of planning on somebody's part for their convenience, if not for that of the general public. Maitland, arriving as he had designed when the hearing was well under way, insinuated himself into a vacant place near the door, though there was plenty of room in what might be considered the well of the court near Sir Nicholas Harding and his learned friend, Miss Vera Langhorne. For that matter, Peter Gibson had also kept a place vacant beside him.

There was today only one magistrate sitting, a woman

74

of whom his first thought was that he wouldn't care to meet her on a dark night. Philip Brady, conspicuous on a chair in the centre of the room, a little isolated from everyone except a uniformed constable, looked uneasy but reasonably calm. That might perhaps be put down to a callous indifference to what he had done, but it wouldn't matter really at a hearing like this where the result was a foregone conclusion and there was no jury to draw the wrong inferences from his demeanour. One man was on his feet, a barrister named Fuller whom Antony recognised from meeting him in the bar mess, and who was evidently conducting the case for the prosecution.

The witness was a big, fair man, a good deal overweight. He was saying, as Antony's attention became focused on him, 'I cautioned him and asked him again where he had been on the night in question, getting the same story that he had given me before. I then showed him the knife, which Doctor Cavanagh has told you he removed from the body of the deceased, upon which he said,' – here the witness made a show of consulting a notebook – ' "that can't be the one, it belongs to me". He was then placed under arrest. I did not question him further until his solicitor was present, when he declined to add anything to what had already been said.'

'About the weapon, Superintendent –' (So this was Superintendent Harley, Peter Gibson's 'man of some compassion'. He looked angry now, and perhaps that was to be expected if he felt that one of his subordinates had let the side down badly.)

'I should explain, for the record,' Harley was saying, 'though of course the weapon has been produced, that it is an oriental dagger of rather unusual design. I certainly have never seen another like it, and I do not think the prisoner could have been mistaken.'

'Your worship,' said Sir Nicholas, rising suddenly to his feet, 'the Superintendent's opinions, however valuable, do not at this moment concern us.' Evidently it wasn't the first time he had intervened. The magistrate took his objection without question.

'You are quite right, Sir Nicholas,' she said smoothly. Maitland's attention wandered for a moment; at least, he heard her voice but what she was saying did not register. He was studying Harley's face with some interest. The Superintendent didn't like the implied rebuke, most likely he didn't like Brady either. There seemed to be some animus there, probably quite unconscious. It would be interesting to know what Brady thought of the Superintendent.

When he brought his mind to bear again on what was being said it was to find that Fuller had finished with the witness and Sir Nicholas was on his feet. 'With your worship's permission – ' The lady inclined her head with something as near graciousness as a rather poker face would allow. 'There are two questions I should like to put to you, Superintendent.' Counsel's tone was smooth as silk. 'The first concerns the book that Mr. Dobell was reading when Mrs. Dobell retired for the night.'

'Barbara Tuchman's *The Proud Tower*,' said Harley, nodding.

'Thank you. I can well understand that he wished to finish it that night, as you told us,' Sir Nicholas went on. 'But tell me, Superintendent, you examined the room before anything was moved?'

'I did.'

'Where was the book then?'

'Face downwards on the couch, beside where the deceased was sitting.'

'As though he had put it down when a visitor arrived?'

'That's what I thought.'

'Then perhaps you can tell me, Superintendent, at what page the book was open.'

There was a dead silence for a moment before Harley said, his confusion very evident, 'That's an odd question, Sir Nicholas.'

'Nevertheless, it is one to which I should like an answer.

76

I might add that if an objection is to be made, it is my learned friend Mr. Fuller's place to make it, not yours.'

Quite definitely, Harley didn't take kindly to criticism. He said, rather sullenly, 'The fact was made a note of, of course. It was open at page two hundred and twenty-six, and the opposite page had a chapter heading, "The Steady Drummer".'

'Do you recall how many pages the book has in all?'

'No.'

'Neither do I precisely, but a good many more than two hundred and twenty-six. Something nearer five hundred. The book was open, presumably, to keep Mr. Dobell's place; about half-way through, was it not?'

'About that.'

'And therefore it cannot be reasonably supposed that he intended to finish it before retiring.'

'I don't see your point, I'm afraid.'

'A small inconsistency, Superintendent. You will do well to bear it in mind. Now my next point is a simple one. You say that Mrs. Dobell telephoned the police when she found her husband dead. At what time was that call received?'

Harley was frowning as though this was another question whose import escaped him. Antony, whose attention was wholly caught now, thought exultantly, 'There's never any need to prime Uncle Nick. He's asking all the questions I wanted to ask the prosecution, and behaving, in spite of his scepticism, exactly as if he believes every word Brady says.' But the moment of optimism didn't last. It was a small point – how very small – about the book, not enough to cast any real doubt on Mrs. Dobell's evidence.

'I believe the record at the station shows that Mrs. Dobell's call was received at ten fifty-five,' said Harley, breaking a silence that had lasted, in fact, no more than a second or two. Counsel said, 'Thank you,' again and sat down, and the tedious business began of getting the witness's statement ready for signature . . . minus, of course, the words that had offended Sir Nicholas. Antony allowed his attention to wander again and for the first time picked out Moira Pershing sitting demurely on a bench a little removed from the general run of the spectators. She was wearing a dress of bottle-green silk, high-necked, long-sleeved, and a matching cap that looked as if it was made of oak leaves, and that did nothing to hide the glory of her hair.

If that was the bench reserved for witnesses, that might be Stephanie Dobell sitting beside her, and she was a smasher too. (Thank goodness Uncle Nick isn't a mind reader; he wouldn't object to the sentiment, being something of a connoisseur himself of female beauty, but he would object to the choice of words.) But her fair good looks were in a way to being extinguished. She was wearing black, a well-cut suit in some summery material, and had a black lace mantilla thrown over her head. Perhaps because of her pallor the colour, which should have suited her, made her look all the more forlorn.

And it seemed he was right in his surmise. A moment later her name had been called and she was on her way to the chair that Superintendent Harley had just vacated. Fuller was on his feet, dealing gently with her, expressing the court's sympathy, eliciting her name, her address, her identification of the deceased as her husband.

The story of Monday evening's events she told in almost the same words as he had heard yesterday from Peter Gibson. (Her demeanour is just right, damn it, the tragic widow bearing up bravely for the sake of avenging her husband's death.) She needed very little prompting, Fuller must have been quite satisfied with his witness. Then she had finished, and turned a little to face Sir Nicholas.

'I should like to associate myself with my learned friend's expressions of regret, madam. I will not detain you, but there is one point I should like you to make quite clear to us. You say you saw my client, Philip Brady, leaving your home on Monday evening. At what time was that . . . exactly?'

'At ten thirty-five.'

'You are sure of that?'

'I looked at the bedroom clock. It keeps very good time.' (And that was a puzzle. If she had understood the import of counsel's questions to the previous witness, surely she would have prevaricated. Unless . . .)

Sir Nicholas showed no signs of dissatisfaction. He said, only, 'Thank you, madam,' and seated himself again, and Antony saw him turn his head to say something to Miss Langhorne. Probably to explain to her exactly what he was getting at, though this seemed neither the time nor the place.

The next witness was not Moira Pershing, as he had expected, but a nondescript-looking man who had been sitting on the widow's other side, and who now gave his name, under Fuller's questioning, as Leslie Simmonds. His address was 33 Temple Street, 'and that, I believe,' said Fuller with some satisfaction evident in his tone, 'is two doors away from the house where the deceased lived with his wife?'

'It is. We had been neighbours for five years.'

'And on Monday evening last, the twenty-fourth of May – '

'I was walking my dog. I generally take him out about ten o'clock and return about half past, but that evening I was a little late. It was ten thirty-five when I was coming up to the Dobells' gate, and I saw a man coming out.'

'Please tell us, Mr. Simmonds, exactly what you saw.'

'I heard footsteps on the path before he came into sight. He pulled the gate open, came through, and then turned and shut it after himself carefully.'

'Was there anything else you noticed about this man?'

'Yes, he was wearing gloves.'

'Do you think you could recognise him again?'

'I'm sure of it. There is a street lamp nearby and I got a good look at his face.'

'Do you see him in this room?'

Every eye in the court must have followed his pointing finger, and there was no doubt at all that he was pointing at the prisoner. Philip, when he realised this, half rose to his feet, and then thought better of it and sank back on to his chair again. Antony saw his uncle get up, without waiting for his opponent to yield place to him. But evidently he had judged the situation correctly; Fuller sat down with a wave of his hand that seemed to say, You're welcome to the witness now.

'It is strange, is it not,' said Sir Nicholas, at his most dulcet, 'that this evidence was not made available to the defence?'

'Mr. Fuller?'

'Your worship, the witness came forward this morning only. There was no time – '

'I think you must accept that, Sir Nicholas.'

'And I have finished with the witness,' said Fuller unnecessarily, sitting down again. 'Thank you, Mr. Simmonds,' he added rather belatedly.

'So long as my protest is noted,' said Sir Nicholas, allowing a tinge of severity to creep into his tone. 'Am I to assume, Mr. Simmonds, that you did not hear of Mr. Dobell's death until this morning?'

'No, I heard what had happened, of course, only I didn't think what I had seen was of any importance.'

'What made you change your mind?'

'I was talking to someone last night who made me see I ought to tell the police. It was late then, so I didn't do anything about it until this morning.'

'Are we to know this "someone's" name?'

'I don't know it myself. I met him in a pub. The Cross Keys,' he added, seeing Sir Nicholas open his mouth for a further query. 'I've seen him there before, but I don't know his name.'

'Then we will turn to your evidence itself, Mr. Simmonds. Have you ever seen my client before today?'

'I saw him on Monday night.'

'But you did not then recognise him?'

'Not until I saw him here this morning.'

'I see. You will forgive me if I question this identification,' said Sir Nicholas. 'A man seen for a moment only . . . but that is for another time and place. How did it come about that you were so sure of the time?' He shot the question at the witness suddenly, and Simmonds was silent for a moment, blinking at him.

'I looked at my watch, under the street lamp I mentioned,' he said at last. 'There was a programme on the telly I wanted to see at ten-thirty, you see, and I was a little late for it.'

'So you were in a hurry,' said Counsel thoughtfully. 'More concerned with getting home than with studying the features of a man you couldn't know was in any way important. I have nothing more to ask the witness,' he added, and sat down.

So they came at last to Moira Pershing. Antony was watching the prisoner when her name was called. Philip remained admirably expressionless, but he followed her with his eyes as she walked across the courtroom and his lips tightened a little. There was the question, of course, of what his feelings were now. He was telling the truth – Maitland believed that firmly – and she had given him the lie direct.

Fuller was being gentle with this witness too. He finished the preliminaries and came to the point without delay. 'One thing only, Miss Pershing. You were with the accused on the evening in question. At what time did he leave you?'

'At ten o'clock. I noticed the time because it was so early, but he said he had a report to write.'

'Thank you, that is all.'

'I am afraid I cannot be quite so commendably brief,' said Sir Nicholas. He was cooing at her too, thought Maitland irreverently. 'You live at Somerset Towers, you say. Is that a furnished or an unfurnished apartment?'

'Furnished.'

'How long have you lived there?'

'Between two and three weeks.'

'You signed a lease?'

'Yes, it was dated the first of May.'

'One year . . . two years?'

'I have the flat on a monthly tenancy.'

81

'You are not employed, I believe you said, Miss Pershing.'

'No. I suppose you'd say I have independent means.'

'You must have had some reason for coming to Northdean.'

'I was at a loose end. I thought it would be a nice place to spend the summer.'

'No friends here?'

'No.' That was said rather quickly.

'Where did you live before?'

'In London.' (And that was vague enough, in all conscience, but Sir Nicholas let it go.)

'So you left your friends – '

'I am unable to see the point of these questions,' said Fuller, jumping up as though a spring had suddenly been released, but he was over-ruled by the magistrate, who seemed to have thawed a little and was showing signs of becoming interested in Sir Nicholas's manoeuvres. Sir Nicholas, however had had enough of the subject.

'You met my client two weeks ago,' he said, a statement rather than a question.

'About that.'

'On the twelfth of May, to be precise.'

'If you say so. I don't remember as exactly as that.'

'When was the arrangement made that you should dine and spend the evening together on May the twenty-fourth?' asked Sir Nicholas, suddenly changing course. Antony, a little resentful – but wasn't he already unduly prejudiced? – thought she showed signs of amusement as she answered.

'I've no particular reason to remember that either. I imagine it was the evening before. We were seeing each other most days by then.'

'You were in fact – are, in fact – engaged to be married to Philip Brady?'

'I think, in the circumstances, perhaps we ought to say "were".'

'You have condemned him so quickly?' This time there was some reproach in his tone, and Moira answered without seeming to take thought.

'I don't like people who tell lies.'

Sir Nicholas ignored that. It was, Antony realised, all he could do in the circumstances, and he began to look forward, without any pleasure at all, to his next conversation with his uncle. 'I wonder if you remember, Miss Pershing, upon what date you consented to marry Philip Brady.'

'Last Sunday.' For the first time she showed some sign of emotion. Maitland, who could not be considered an unbiased observer, thought cynically, She's remembered she's supposed to be fond of him.

'The twenty-third of May?'

'I suppose so. Yes, of course, it must have been.'

'Thank you, madam, that is all.'

And that was the end of the prosecution's case . . . and quite enough too, Antony considered. Harley must be very sure of himself to have introduced the new witness, Simmonds, without even the formality of an identification parade; but if it had been a gamble it was one that had handsomely paid off. No good waiting for the rest of the formalities, the end was a foregone conclusion. There was a place across the road where he could get a sandwich and be ready in good time to accompany Peter Gibson to the prison.

IV

As the court emptied, Sir Nicholas looked about for his nephew, but when it became apparent that he was not among those present he took his leave of Peter Gibson, took Vera Langhorne firmly in charge, and summoned a taxi to take them back to the Red Lion. 'You will allow me the pleasure of giving you luncheon,' he said, as soon as they were settled and the driver had been given his instructions. And added, when he thought his companion was hesitating over her reply, 'There are things I wish to discuss with you.'

'Glad to,' said Vera, in her usual terse way. And then, practically, 'There's a bus back to Chedcombe every hour.'

'Well, as to that . . . but we will discuss it over our meal,' said Sir Nicholas. She gathered from his gesture that he did not wish to speak while the driver could certainly hear them.

'Plenty of time,' she agreed.

It was getting late and they were given a table in the corner. Sir Nicholas surveyed the almost empty room with satisfaction, but he did not attempt to speak until the important question of what they were going to eat and drink had been decided and the waiter had departed with their order. Then he said, smiling at his companion, 'I would not have you think that my conduct of the case this morning in any way represented my own idea of what should be done.'

Vera frowned at him. 'Very effective,' she said.

'Yes, but at this stage – '

'Tactics,' said Vera, nodding as though satisfied with her interpretation of his remark.

'Precisely. I should very much have preferred to leave my questions until the trial. They could do no good, Brady was bound to be committed, but in view of Antony's desire to clear the matter up without delay I felt bound to do what I could to help him.'

'Very natural.'

'Now, there I have to disagree with you. But he cannot himself approach the prosecution witnesses, and I felt there were things he would wish to know.' He was interrupted there by the waiter returning with their wine; he sat back in his chair, sipped, nodded his approval, and did not speak again until the wine was poured and they were alone. 'I must admit,' he said then, a trifle ruefully, 'to an unregenerate feeling that, having gone so far with my cross-examination, I should have liked the opportunity to go the whole way. There are certain inconsistencies – '

'Coming around to Antony's way of thinking,' said Vera.

'Not entirely. What did you make of our client, Miss Langhorne?'

'Think he was more hurt and bewildered than anything else. By that girl letting him down,' she amplified, when he looked at her enquiringly. 'If he's going to be frightened by his predicament, that will come later.'

'Now that is a very acute observation.' Sir Nicholas sounded thoughtful. 'Do you realise, I wonder, that you are at least half-way to believing this preposterous story of Antony's?'

Vera drank some of her wine and said, as she had said earlier that day, 'Been right before.'

'That's true. That's why I feel bound to give him his head,' Sir Nicholas told her. 'He is concerned that there shouldn't be a miscarriage of justice, and of course if there is any question of that – '

'Know what you mean,' said Miss Langhorne, when he let the sentence trail into silence.

'It is because of that possibility that I am emboldened to make a request of you.' He paused, not looking at her; twirling the wine glass, in fact, and watching the way the wine swirled with the movement. 'I am seriously worried about this case, Miss Langhorne. Antony has taken it very much to heart, and in view of what he believes I do not feel it right to discourage him, even if I thought I could do so.'

'Quite see that.'

'But if he is right . . . *if* he is right,' Sir Nicholas repeated doubtfully, 'Brady is innocent and the rest of the witnesses are lying. That argues strongly in favour of a wide-spread organisation . . . for the existence of this Mr. X, in fact.'

'Thinking of the danger. That's why you're staying,' said Vera, in the triumphant tone of one who has solved a tricky problem.

'That is true. And I can quite see that it is better not to delay the investigation. If there is danger, the sooner matters are brought to a head the better. But I want to know what is happening, I want to be with him every step of the way. And – this is where I want to trespass on your kindness, Miss Langhorne – I should like to feel you are taking a similar interest. I have come to rely on your judgment – '

'Kindness doesn't come into it. Fond of him,' said Miss

85

Langhorne, perhaps even more gruffly than usual. Sir Nicholas beamed at her.

'Then we can consider that settled,' he said with satisfaction.

'You'll keep me posted – '

'I don't mean that exactly. I am hoping that you will come back to town with us for the weekend – I have spoken to Jenny, and she is looking forward to seeing you – and perhaps we shall hear something of this idea of Antony's when he has spoken to Roger Farrell.'

That reduced Vera altogether to silence for a moment. 'If you're sure – ' she said at last.

'Quite sure. Jenny will be telephoning you at home tonight.'

'Then I'll be glad to come. Quite see your point about the danger. Better than waiting for news,' said Vera. Sir Nicholas might have been about to express his pleasure at getting his own way, but at that moment the waiter came back with a laden tray.

V

Maitland walked back to the hotel after he had finished his coffee and sandwiches, because that was the best place to pick up a cab. He arrived at the Gibsons' when Peter was just about to start his own luncheon, and was given a seat by the empty fireplace so that they could converse as the meal progressed. Peter was inclined to be apologetic, which was unnecesary in the circumstances, but was silenced on that score by Antony's explanation that he had left the hearing early.

'I didn't know you were there,' said Peter, pausing with his fork half-way to his mouth. 'I kept a seat for you.'

'I didn't want to be any more conspicuous than I could help.'

Peter had a sharp glance for that, but he said only, 'No,

86

of course not,' and left the subject there. Again there were no children present and Antony wondered vaguely whether they were still at school, or grown-up and at work, but this didn't seem the time to ask. Lucy always took it for granted that he knew all about them. Now, not unnaturally, she was full of talk about the murder and Brady's arrest. She didn't seem to share her husband's opinion – probably he had never expressed it to her – but was loud in condemnation of police stupidity. Peter said nothing to contradict her so most likely, Antony felt, his first idea had been right and the solicitor had decided, in the interests of domestic peace, to keep his ideas to himself.

So the meal passed tranquilly enough. 'We don't have to go out to the prison,' Peter said as he pushed back his chair. 'The authorities agreed to keep Brady in the cells at the police station until you could talk to him. We can use one of the interview rooms there.'

'Well, that's something to be thankful for, at any rate,' said Antony, who hated prison visiting perhaps more than any other activity. But there would still be locked doors, and the knowledge that Philip Brady wasn't free any longer to come and go as he pleased. And that thought was a waste of time, if ever there was one. He shook himself free of it and got up to follow Peter out to the car. 'Though I needn't have come here if I'd known,' he said, 'and made you rush your lunch.'

'Never mind. The sooner we get started the better,' said Peter. And then, perhaps sensing the uneasiness of the other man's mood, 'I could tell you, of course, everything that Philip said to us this morning.'

'I'd rather hear it from him, if you don't mind. Though I admit,' he added, smiling, 'this isn't the sort of errand I enjoy.'

'Just as you like.'

'There is also the fact that your own . . . prejudice . . . might colour what you told me.'

Peter drew up, rather jerkily, at the 'Stop' sign at the end of the road, but he made no direct comment. 'What does Sir Nicholas think?' he asked.

'You ought to be able to tell me that. I haven't seen him since the hearing.'

'He didn't commit himself either way, but I thought from the questions he asked –'

'That was for my benefit. Didn't some of the answers make you think?'

'The evidence was, and remains, very strong. I wish I agreed with you, Antony. You're going to find Philip in a pretty pessimistic mood,' he added, wrenching the subject forcibly into a different vein.

'I didn't expect anything else,' Maitland told him, and lapsed into an unhappy silence.

And that was the first thing he thought when Brady was ushered into the interview room and the door clanged behind him . . . that Gibson had been a true prophet. Perhaps Philip had been guarding his expression in the courtroom, but there was very little pretence now. He looked haggard and uncertain of himself and his voice shook a little when he said, neglecting to greet his visitors, 'You're my last hope, Mr. Maitland. I suppose you realise that.'

'It's early days yet,' said Antony vaguely. It couldn't be said that he liked the reminder that he had taken on himself a responsibility that he might not be able to discharge. 'We'd better sit down, hadn't we?' he added.

Brady did take a chair then, at the end of the long table, but he didn't look as if he was paying much attention to what was said. 'Not that I'm not grateful to Sir Nicholas,' he remarked. 'If anyone can make bricks without straw I should think he can. But I don't quite understand, in the face of the evidence, what you think can be done.'

'We shall try, Peter and I, to provide the straw my uncle so badly needs.' That was said lightly and Philip flushed, as though he thought some sarcasm had been intended.

'I mean . . . there it is!' he said. 'How can you possibly believe me?'

'It isn't what I believe that matters,' said Maitland, as he had said it perhaps a hundred times to clients in the past. But then he relented. 'Though, as a matter of fact, I do believe you.'

There was a moment of silence, while Brady's eyes searched his face. Perhaps he was doubtful whether Counsel was in earnest. 'And the witnesses?' he asked at last.

'Bribery . . . intimidation.' Maitland was vague again. 'Did Peter explain to you that I know something of the background of the diamond smuggling racket in this town?'

'He said there was a case, six years ago – '

'Then we needn't go into it again. I suppose you could say that predisposed me to believe you.'

'About the wrongful arrest case . . . yes, I understand that. But Harley believed me about that and now he thinks – '

'Let's forget about Superintendent Harley for the moment and take a look at the evidence,' Antony suggested. And we'll start with the most difficult part, he thought, though this he did not say aloud. 'About your alibi – '

Brady looked down at his hands which were clenched in front of him, and which had made smear marks in the dust on the table-top. 'There is no explanation I can give you,' he said. And then, as though he could no longer contain himself, 'She didn't even try to sound sorry for what she was doing to me!'

There was really nothing to be said to that. Antony didn't try. 'You are quite definite that it was half-past midnight when you left Miss Pershing?' he said.

'Of course I am!'

'Forgive me. I'm not implying that you might have killed Dobell after all, you know, but I must be sure I have your story correct in every detail.'

'I can see that.' He glanced at Peter Gibson as though seeking guidance, and then said, turning back to Maitland again, 'I can only assure you – '

'We'll take it as read then.' He hesitated a little, considering the wording of his next question. 'Miss Pershing did not strike me as the sort of girl who would lie out of a mistaken sense of propriety.'

'If you mean, would she be afraid people would be shocked at our being together in her flat until such a late hour . . . well, all I can say is, she wouldn't have considered it for a moment. Damn it all, she didn't come out of the ark.'

'So I supposed.' Maitland smiled at him, and this time Brady smiled back with something like real amusement.

'For some reason, that's what you wanted to hear,' he said.

'I'm as capable as the next man of becoming wedded to a theory,' Antony admitted. 'Look here, tell me what you know about her.'

'Very little more than Sir Nicholas elicited from her in court.' He paused, glanced at Peter again, and then said in a rush, 'I can tell you how she seemed to me, amusing, even witty, a little caustic sometimes at other people's expense . . . no reason to doubt that side of her is genuine. But the other side, the side nobody but me saw . . . she was loving, and – and responsive, and damnably attractive. I still can't believe that it was a fake.'

'I think we have to face the fact, Mr. Brady, that her acquaintance with you was contrived. Not perhaps with this particular plan in view – '

'I know you must be right, but I can't for the life of me see why.'

'Because in some way you were endangering the whole organisation that Mr. X has built up.'

'Peter explained that to me, but if he's got his tracks as well covered as you say I don't see how I could possibly have been a threat to him.'

'One thing leads to another. For instance, when Dobell and Irving were acquitted did you intend to drop the matter?'

'No, I didn't. Of course, they were out of trouble, but the way the evidence went . . . the way it just dissolved before our eyes . . . I felt there must be someone behind them. I wanted to know who it was.'

'Who knew of this?'

'Why, everyone at the station, I should think. I certainly made no secret of the fact.'

'I see. When did you meet Miss Pershing?'

'On the twelfth of May, as Sir Nicholas said in court.'

'How did that come about?'

'I went round to the Coach and Horses, it's just round the corner from my place – '

'Do you often go there?'

'Most nights, if I haven't a date. Unless I'm on duty, of course.'

'If the meeting was contrived – '

'Well, I'll agree, from that point of view it could have been. But she was there when I went in; I thought at first she was waiting for somebody. And later . . . I'll swear I made all the running.'

Maitland smiled openly at that. 'I'd be surprised if you told me anything else,' he said. 'You didn't add "clever", or "full of feminine wiles", to your list of her qualities, but I think we can take it that both attributes are there all right. About your engagement – '

'I never meant to ask her to marry me, I hope you believe that. Not until the case was settled and I knew where I stood. Only somehow – ' He looked from one of his companions to the other and smiled rather wryly. 'You're going to say more feminine wiles,' he said.

'Something like that,' Maitland agreed. 'But we'll leave Miss Pershing for the moment. What do you know of Mrs. Dobell?'

'They're not . . . they weren't a devoted couple, though in a sense Dobell seemed like an indulgent husband. He certainly spent money on her lavishly, and I should say that was what kept them together. She stayed for what she could get out of him, and he – well, perhaps he had a certain pride of possession. She's a good looker, you saw that for yourself this morning.'

'Did it occur to you . . . did you suspect she knew anything about the diamond smuggling?'

'She seemed very indignant that the charge was made. I think she really believed that her husband was innocent.'

'Therefore she resented you? Even if it was just that she thought you were interfering with her meal ticket.'

'But that isn't enough to explain – '

'No, I don't think it is. It wouldn't have made her any harder to convince where her best interests lay though, would it?'

'I suppose not. But do you think even Sir Nicholas could persuade her to say in court that she's lying?'

'I hope that won't be necessary.'

'Do you really think – ?'

'Don't ask me what I think!' The retort came swiftly, almost savagely; Maitland was beginning to realise just what he had taken on. Peter Gibson gave him a curious look, but Philip said, as though he had noticed nothing,

'I can't throw any light on the other evidence, either. The Simmonds man, I mean. I never saw or heard of him before.'

'I didn't suppose you could.' Antony's tone was completely normal again. 'You can help me about the knife, however. Is there any chance you were mistaken about its being yours?'

'No. It's a dagger-like thing I use as a paper-knife. I couldn't possibly mistake it. It came from abroad somewhere, I've an uncle who used to be a ship's purser.'

'Then – '

'I can't explain.'

'You can tell me when you last saw it, who had an opportunity of taking it. That shouldn't be too difficult.'

Brady gave him an odd look. 'Do you want me to tell you the truth?'

'For heaven's sake, don't start lying to me. Things are bad enough without that.'

'Yes, but this only makes matters worse, you see. I used it to open my mail on Monday morning.'

'Are you sure about that?' Antony's tone had sharpened again.

'Quite sure.'

92

'Did you always use it? Had it become a matter of habit?'

'Don't you see, that's why I am sure? I use it every morning, I couldn't possibly have helped noticing if it wasn't there.'

'Perhaps you had no post that morning.'

'There was a letter from the Bank saying my current account wasn't in very good shape. I know it was that day because I dealt with the matter immediately . . . in the morning, before I saw you.'

'I see. Did you see the dagger after that?'

'No. I had no occasion to notice whether it was still there or not.'

'Well then, who was in the flat during the day?'

'My cleaning woman has a key, but it wasn't her day for going in. All the same – '

'Peter and I were with you later in the day . . . and Miss Pershing.'

'But she couldn't . . . we were together the whole time. She never even went near the writing-table.'

'You came into the hall to let us in. I venture to suggest that your attention was fully occupied for the moment . . . in summing up, let us say.'

Brady grinned at that, but his eyes were thoughtful. 'That's true, of course. I was curious to see what sort of a fish Peter had landed.'

Maitland laughed. He seemed to have relaxed again now. 'I hope you were satisfied,' he said lightly. And then, 'You do see my point, don't you? She had plenty of time and her handbag was quite large enough – '

'I see that all right. And I suppose it's no worse, believing she'd steal the knife, than knowing she lied about the time I left her.' He paused and then added, as though the idea had come to him suddenly and startled him, 'You don't think that she – ?'

'I think her part in the affair went no further than helping to incriminate you. With a stabbing intended, a man would

93

be a more efficient tool. But there's somebody in Northdean manipulating events.'

'Mr. X's representative?'

'Yes. My guess is he's a local man . . . and I could give you a score of reasons for that opinion, Peter,' he said, when Gibson seemed about to break his silence. 'One will perhaps suffice. Somebody knew a good deal about Inspector Brady, even before Miss Pershing got here.'

'It does seem logical, I suppose,' said Peter slowly. 'Somebody who was manipulating Irving and Dobell too, and who finally killed Dobell.'

'I think so, yes.' He turned back to Philip again. 'I'm hoping to see John Irving later today,' he said. 'That should be interesting. From some points of view he's a logical suspect. I mean, he might have been persuaded into adding murder to his other activities.'

'It looks to me like an insoluble problem,' said Philip dejectedly. 'Frankly, I don't see where you're going to begin.'

Maitland got up, startling the others by the suddenness of his movement. 'We'd better be getting on with it,' he said. 'And it isn't the beginning that's difficult, Philip, because I've got a sort of idea. But bringing matters to a satisfactory conclusion is another matter.'

Brady ignored that. 'What sort of an idea?' he demanded.

'A nebulous one,' Antony told him. There was something in his tone that precluded further questioning. 'I want to talk to Sergeant Cummings and Constable Peach,' he went on. 'Do you suppose we'll be lucky enough to find them in the station?'

Philip was beginning, 'I don't know – ' when Peter Gibson got up in his turn and said briskly.

'I'll find out. You know that isn't how I hoped the interview would go,' he added, when a uniformed constable had taken Brady away, 'but you're beginning to infect me with some of your confidence.'

Antony looked at him in silence for a moment. Then,

'Confident,' he said, 'doesn't exactly describe my state of mind.'

'You've a confidence in Philip's innocence that I wish I shared.'

'Yes, I expect he noticed you took very little part in our talk, don't you?'

'I can't help that. Look here, Antony, I'm backing you up as well as I know how – '

'I realise that.'

' – but I'm beginning to wonder whether it wasn't a mistake bringing Sir Nicholas into the affair at all.'

'Believe me, Uncle Nick is a much more competent advocate than I am.'

'But this question of sincerity . . . as I said, yours is damned convincing.'

'If Uncle Nick isn't convinced himself by the time the trial comes on, the jury will be the last people to know it, I can assure you.'

'I dare say you're right. Well, come along,' said Peter, as if his companion had been the one who was delaying their departure. 'We'll see if those two people you want to see are in.'

VI

They were half-way lucky. Constable Peach was off duty, but they found Sergeant Cummings at his desk and took him back to the interview room with them for the sake of privacy. Maitland thought he went with them unwillingly, certainly his manner was uneasy. That was probably because – might as well admit it – his own reputation had gone before him. Something might be deduced from it . . . a guilty conscience, perhaps. But that was carrying guesswork a little far.

'A good steady type,' Peter had said, and that – discounting the nervousness – was just what he seemed: a burly man, round-faced, with a rather high complexion. 'I don't know

95

anything about the case against Inspector Brady,' he said, as soon as they were alone together. 'Nothing to do with me.'

'We realise that. It's about the earlier case,' said Peter soothingly. 'The action for wrongful arrest that was brought against the Inspector.'

'I wasn't a witness,' said Cummings rather hurriedly.

'No,' said Antony, thinking it was time he took a hand. 'But you were in charge of one of the keys to the filing cabinet from which the witnesses' statements disappeared.'

'Oh, that!' Suddenly he seemed more confident. 'The cabinet in question was in Inspector Brady's office, you know. As for the lock, I could have opened it myself with a paper clip.'

'I suspected as much. But I'd still like to know if anyone else, at any time, had access to the key.'

'It was out of my possession.'

'You seem very sure of that.'

'I am sure. It came up before, when the statements went missing, so naturally I've given it some thought.'

'Where do you keep the key?'

'With those of the other cabinets, on a separate ring from my own keys.'

'And when one of your colleagues needs something – ?'

'I open the cabinet for him myself. If you're thinking someone could have taken out the statements in my presence, but without my knowledge, think again. It couldn't have been done.'

'That wasn't . . . exactly . . . what was in my mind. In which pocket did you carry the keys?'

'Trouser pocket. I might take my jacket off, see, if it was hot in the office, then someone might have taken the keys and me none the wiser. But that couldn't have happened.'

'At home – '

'My wife and kids?' He sounded scornful. 'You're not thinking of one of them?'

'Nothing like that. But you're in the uniform branch,

96

Sergeant, and presumably you don't wear your uniform off duty. If the keys were still in the pocket of your uniform and were left at home – '

'Look, I'm responsible for those cabinets. I keep the keys with me, on duty or off.'

'And if somebody needs something from them when you're not at the station – ?'

'They'd call me in, if it were urgent enough. But that doesn't often happen. Mostly papers aren't put away until they're finished with, at least for the time being. No one unauthorised is likely to get into the station, you see.'

'I see. What do you think happened to the statements, Sergeant?'

'Well, sir, it's not for me to say. Whoever it was didn't get into the cabinet with my key, that's all I can tell you.'

'Do you remember the statements being put away?'

'Yes, I do. Young Peach brought them to me, they *looked* all right and proper – '

'What did you think, Sergeant, when the case against Dobell and Irving started to go awry?'

'I thought there'd been some funny business, sir.'

'Yes, but on whose part?'

'If the statements were fakes after all – '

'I see. You think Inspector Brady was framing the two accused.'

'That's not for me to say.'

And that was all that was to be got out of him. 'Though it's obvious what he thinks,' said Peter as they left the police station together a few minutes later. 'Philip was wrong when he said his colleagues believed him about the first case.'

'I should point out to you,' said Antony, falling into step beside him, 'that the worthy Sergeant doesn't necessarily believe what he told us ... or rather implied.'

'N-no.' Gibson sounded doubtful. 'I don't see that talking to him did the slightest good, anyway.'

'It might do if I came to think that he was responsible for the removal of the statements himself.'

97

'Do you think that?' Peter demanded.

'I think the possibility is worth bearing in mind.' But when Gibson tried to pursue the subject he seemed disinclined for further speculation. 'What's next on the agenda?' he asked.

'You want to see Irving.'

'Yes, but for some reason I feel it would be more constructive to talk to him and his wife together. That means waiting until he's home from work.'

'About half past five, unless he's doing overtime.'

'That probably doesn't arise now that, presumably, the shipment of diamonds has been suspended. Suppose we go back to the hotel, Peter, and order some tea, and ask them to bring it to us in the bar. Would Noyes be on duty?'

Gibson glanced at his watch. 'Just about,' he said. 'He comes on at four o'clock.'

'We'll do that then.' Maitland was suddenly confident. 'He may even,' he said, quickening his pace, 'have something positive to tell us.'

VII

He had expected to find his uncle already drinking tea, but when they went into the larger of the hotel lounges there was no sign of Sir Nicholas. The waiter arrived promptly, received his instructions without apparent surprise, and Antony and Peter followed him out of the room and went across the hall to the bar. This was a cheerful place with windows looking out on the square; old fashioned, as the hotel itself was old fashioned, with lots of well polished wood and really comfortable chairs. Maitland ignored these, however, and went and perched on one of the tall stools at the bar. Gibson followed his example and the barman looked at them expectantly.

'Nothing for us,' said Antony. He did not seem to be in a mood to waste words. 'Are you Edward Noyes?'

'Yes, I am.' Noyes was a big man with a pasty complexion and hands that looked too clumsy for the delicate work of bar-tending. 'As Mr. Gibson very well knows,' he added. His tone was faintly surly.

'We want to talk to you,' said Antony. He glanced deliberately round the room, though he had noted as he came in that it was empty. 'As you don't seem to be too busy – '

'I suppose you're this lawyer chap from London that everyone's talking about.'

Peter knew his companion well enough by now to glance at him anxiously, but Antony's tone was equable when he replied. 'My name's Maitland. I'm . . . concerned with Inspector Brady's defence.'

'If you want to talk about him murdering Mr. Dobell, *I* can't help you. I know nothing about it.'

Their tea arrived then, and there was a pause while the elderly waiter placed cups and teapot before them. When he had gone Antony did not speak immediately, but watched Peter pouring the tea as though there was some fascination in this simple task. Then he said, with a quick upward glance at Noyes, 'You might know enough to make a guess who had arranged to frame him.'

That brought a moment's dead silence. Then Noyes said, blustering, 'What do you mean? I don't know . . . you must be mad to talk like that.'

'Yes, perhaps I should spell it out for you,' said Maitland reflectively. 'I mean that it was probably the same person who – shall we say? – arranged for you to change your evidence when Dobell and Irving were on trial.'

' 'Ere!' It was a heartfelt cry, and Antony obliged by fixing his eyes on the barman's face. 'You're accusing me of lying,' said Noyes aggressively.

'How acute of you to realise that.' Anyone who knew them both would have seen the elusive likeness to Sir Nicholas very marked at that moment. 'You haven't denied it, you know,' he went on.

'Of course I deny it!'

'Tell me then, your connection with the case.'

'Why should I?'

'To convince me, perhaps, that I'm wrong.'

'They called me to give evidence. I was on oath, wasn't I? I had to tell the truth, didn't I? That's all there was to it.'

'You forget, I wasn't in court.'

'*He*'ll have told you.' Noyes's glance in Gibson's direction held something of viciousness. 'I've seen them both in the bar sometimes, Dobell and Irving, but never together. Not that I remember.'

'I see. You're asking us to believe,' said Maitland speaking slowly and giving every word its weight, 'that Inspector Brady questioned you, that you told him what you have just told us, and that in spite of this you were called to give evidence for the prosecution.'

'That's how it was,' said Noyes, still aggressive. But there were beads of sweat round his hairline and on his upper lip; he was obviously very far from being happy at the way the conversation was going.

And suddenly Maitland had had enough. 'I'll bring the cups if you'll carry the teapot, Peter,' he said, sliding off his stool. 'We'll be more comfortable in the other room.'

VIII

Sir Nicholas was still absent when they went through into the lounge. Antony, going ahead of his companion, chose chairs by the window, with a table conveniently to hand, a little removed from the other residents who were clustered, for some reason, round the empty hearth.

'I don't know what good you think that did,' said Peter as he seated himself.

'I made him sweat a little,' said Antony with satisfaction. 'Well, yes, but – '

'I didn't mean literally, though that's true enough. I meant that he might be the weak link in the chain, Peter. If we scared him sufficiently – '

'There wasn't much "we" about it. Quite frankly, it would never have occurred to me to attack him openly like that.' It was obvious from Gibson's tone that he was registering a protest, though he didn't say so in so many words.

'That's because you haven't thought of all the possibilities,' Antony assured him. 'If he's sufficiently scared he may run to his master, and the result might be . . . well, illuminating.'

Peter thought about that for a moment. 'I see your point,' he said at last. And added bluntly, 'But it won't help Philip if you get yourself killed.'

'I don't imagine anything quite so drastic will happen without orders from on high,' said Maitland. His tone was flippant but there was no amusement in his eyes. 'I'm after the missing link, Peter, the chap who pulls the strings on Mr. X's behalf . . . the only person in Northdean, in all probability, who knows who Mr. X is.'

'Is that all?' said Gibson in a rather hollow voice.

'It will do to be going on with. And while we're about it, there's something you can do for me. I want enquiries made into Moira Pershing's background.'

'That's something I can take care of.' Gibson sounded relieved. Then he glanced at his watch. 'Half an hour yet before we can go to the Irvings,' he said. 'You might tell me, do you intend to insult them too?'

Antony passed his cup for a refill. 'I shall play it by ear,' he said virtuously, 'and do whatever the situation seems to require.'

IX

Sir Nicholas still hadn't reappeared when they left, and though Antony tried his room from the phone in the hall there was no reply. The Irvings lived in a part of the town that was strange to him, though they passed Orchard Close, where the Barnards lived, on the way. Their destination was a terrace house, solidly built and quite large, with a handsome bow window to the right of the front door. And they had been a little too eager. John Irving had only just arrived home and wasn't pleased to see them. His wife, Doris, a pretty, fair-haired woman who wore too much make-up, let them in and took them immediately into the living-room where her husband was relaxing with a generous shot of what looked like neat whisky.

'Mr. Gibson,' said Doris. 'You've heard of Mr. Gibson. And a Mr. Maitland, who says he's a lawyer too.'

Irving scowled, and did not attempt to get up to greet the visitors. 'What do they want?' he demanded.

'To talk to you.'

'To you both,' corrected Peter gently before Maitland could open his mouth. Antony had an amused look for that, evidently the solicitor didn't altogether trust his good intentions, but Irving's attention for the moment seemed riveted on the man he knew, by the name at least, so no harm was done.

'What about then?' Irving was still truculent.

'First of all, we'd like to know what your intentions are in the matter of the case you were bringing against Philip Brady.'

'You needn't have come all this way just for that, I should have thought. He killed that when he killed Cliff Dobell.'

'Then you don't intend to institute proceedings on your own?'

'What's the use. He's up for murder, isn't he? I don't suppose he could afford to pay me damages; *and* his lawyers,' he added, with a disagreeable look in Antony's direction. 'Take him for all he's got, I wouldn't wonder.'

Maitland smiled, and decided it was time he took some part in the conversation. In deference to Peter's feelings, however, he'd start on a low key. 'Do you agree with that decision, Mrs. Irving?' he enquired.

She was still standing by the fireplace, with one hand

clenched and resting on the mantel. Instead of answering she said, rather jerkily, 'You'd better sit down, both of you. And can I get you anything to drink?'

'Nothing, thank you.' Peter answered for them both. After, a moment, when they still remained standing, she went to the chair at the other side of the hearth from her husband, seated herself, and picked up the sherry glass that stood waiting at her elbow.

'Then you won't mind if we go on with ours,' she said. 'We always have a drink when Johnny gets home.'

Maitland and Gibson had sat down side by side on the sofa, and Maitland was taking in the furnishings of the room, which was quite as large as the exterior of the house suggested. Everything looked newish, but you couldn't fault it for that. Looking at Doris he would have expected her taste to run to the flashy; in fact, the decor was rather subdued, and he liked it the better for that.

Peter was saying, rather lamely, 'We don't want to disturb you,' which as far as his colleague was concerned was a downright lie. It was time to get things moving.

'You didn't answer my question, Mrs. Irving,' Antony reminded her.

'I don't remember – '

'How do you feel about your husband's decision not to proceed against Inspector Brady?'

'Well, I agree with it, of course. It wouldn't do any good, would it, when the man's in prison already?'

'Tell me about the case.' He was still addressing the woman, and she glanced at her husband uncertainly.

'I don't see what concern it is of yours, now that I've told you I'm not going on with it,' Irving growled.

'The position is perhaps a little difficult for a layman to understand,' said Maitland airily. 'If you were going on with it we should have left by now; I shouldn't have anything to say to you until we met in court. As it is, we need your help.'

'Why should I – ?'

'Mr. Gibson is Inspector Brady's solicitor – '

'I know that.'

'– and I am associated with him in the preparation of the defence.'

'You're talking about murder now. I know nothing about it.'

'Yet the prosecution's case will rest to some degree on the fact that the deceased was a party to the action being brought against our client. That's supposed to give him a motive,' he explained, looking again at Doris. She was sipping her drink, but her eyes met his anxiously above the glass.

'Of course it gives him a motive.' Irving sounded contemptuous.

'We must agree to differ about that.' Maitland's tone was still smooth as silk and Peter Gibson was beginning to look worried. 'Why were you bringing the case, Mr. Irving?' Antony went on.

Irving paused to refresh himself before he answered that. 'A matter of principle,' he said then, a little smugly. 'Only right – wasn't it? – when the case against us wouldn't stand up.'

'The question is, should it have stood up?'

'Of course not.' That was said casually, without emphasis. Irving got up, refilled his own glass and his wife's and came back to his chair again.

'You're not denying that diamonds were being shipped from Hargreaves & Company's plant?'

'So the police say.'

Maitland chose to take that as agreement. 'Then don't you think that perhaps Dobell – ?'

'No, I don't! He was innocent, same as me. Do you think he'd have joined with me in prosecuting this Brady of yours if he hadn't been?'

'I think, if you will pardon my saying so, Mr. Irving, that you were both acting under instructions.'

'I don't know what you mean.'

'So the question is, you see, who gave you those

instructions? Do you know, Mrs. Irving?' he asked, turning to her suddenly.

'Don't you go trying to drag Doris into this.' Irving's tone held a spitefulness that hadn't been there before. Doris was staring at Maitland rather as if she had seen a snake in her path. 'Hinting things won't get you anywhere,' said Irving. 'Say it straight out, why don't you?'

'There's really no need. I think we understand each other very well,' said Antony dulcetly. He was using his uncle's tactics, an unashamed bit of plagiarism because he was quite unconscious of it. 'I've only two more questions for you, and then we'll leave you in peace. Or perhaps not,' he added, and again looked deliberately in Doris Irving's direction.

'At least, we'll be glad to see the back of you.' Irving seemed resolved on keeping Maitland's attention focused on himself. 'What are these questions then?' he added. His voice had gone down the scale until it was a growl again.

'The first is, have you worked any overtime lately?'

'What the hell has that got to do with you?'

'Has he, Mrs. Irving?'

'I – no, it's been lovely,' said Doris. 'He's been home every night.'

'Shut up, can't you?' Irving was on his feet. 'I don't know where you think you get off,' he added heatedly. 'We're not answering any more of your questions.'

'That's a pity, because the last one is the most important. Aren't you at least interested to hear what it is?'

'Go ahead if you want to. I'm not answering, and neither is she.'

'Here it is then. Quite simple really. Where were you, Mr. Irving, between ten and ten thirty last Monday evening?'

Speaking simultaneously, Irving said violently, 'Get out of here!' and Doris said, a note of fear in her voice, 'You ought to answer that, Johnny. He was here, Mr. Maitland, with me.'

X

Peter Gibson was silent as they made their way back to the hotel again. Maitland gave him a quizzical look as they went into the hall. 'I need a drink,' he said, 'and don't tell me it's too early. Or are you too annoyed to join me?'

'I never said – '

'No, but it's sticking out all over you like a porcupine's quills. Come into the bar, there's a good chap. Or do you think Noyes will poison us if we give him the chance?'

'I shouldn't wonder. Well, I shouldn't altogether blame him,' said Peter, but he turned his steps obligingly towards the door of the bar. 'I must admit, Antony, I didn't expect anything quite like the series of interviews you've involved me in today.'

Maitland made no comment on that, but led the way to a table in the far corner. There was a waitress on duty now, and he ordered 'Two Black Labels . . . doubles,' without consulting his companion, and then turned to him with the oddly diffident look he sometimes displayed. 'I hope that's all right for you.'

'Quite all right. Like you, I need it,' said Peter emphatically. 'I don't know what idea you've got into your head – '

'Let me ask you one thing. Noyes, for instance, and Irving. What did you expect me to ask them?'

'I . . . well, come to think of it, I haven't the faintest idea.'

Antony glanced up at the bar, where Noyes was busying himself with bottle and glasses, at the same time carefully ignoring their presence. 'Tell me,' he said, 'what did you make of the Irvings? You saw him in court, of course, when he and Dobell were charged with diamond smuggling.'

'Yes, I attended, as I told you, out of interest. Philip had talked about the case a good deal. But I knew both the defendants by sight anyway, as they seemed to know me. Northdean's like that.' He broke off as the waitress came back with a tray, and while she was serving them noticed for the first time the look of strain on his companion's face, and the awkward way he held himself. Jenny, or Sir Nicholas, or any of their close friends, would have known at once that Antony's shoulder was troubling him, but none of them would have commented on the fact. Peter, genuinely concerned, said sharply as soon as the waitress was out of earshot again, 'Antony, is anything wrong?'

'Nothing at all. What should there be?' Maitland's tone had its sharpness too. 'Except that I wish Brady were here having a drink with us, instead of being in that damn prison.' He picked up his glass and raised it a little. 'To freedom,' he said, and drank.

Some instinct warned Peter not to pursue the subject. He added water to his whisky, admired the colour for a moment, and then said, 'I'm sorry if I was querulous when we came in. I realise you know much more about this kind of thing than I do.'

'Perhaps I should have warned you . . . never mind that! You were going to give me your impressions of the Irvings.'

'He's a hard nut. She was nervous, perhaps understandably.'

Surprisingly, Antony laughed. 'You mean, in face of the big, bad wolf from London?'

Peter smiled too. 'Something like that,' he acknowledged. At the same time he was conscious, without understanding it at all, of a feeling of relief, as though a crisis of some sort had been passed. 'Antony . . . are we right about them?'

'You said you believed Brady about the case against Irving and Dobell.' Maitland's tone was flat, he was careful to keep any hint of accusation out of it.

'Well, so I did. So I do. This is a damnable business,' said Peter.

'I admit, they weren't quite what I expected from what you told me of the gossip in the town. He seemed to be the dominant character, but whatever he's up to I'd say she was in it up to the neck. He tried to keep my attention fixed on himself, and I can't decide whether that was out of consideration for her or because he knows she's a compulsive talker and would answer at length if given half the chance.'

'Then you really think – ?'

'I said so, didn't I? You told me they weren't living above their income, Peter, but they're certainly doing themselves well. There was nothing cheap about the house, or the furniture, and he was drinking Laphroaig and she was drinking Bristol Cream.'

'What the devil is Laph-what-you-said?'

'A rather special whisky that Uncle Nick happens to keep in the house because Bruce Halloran likes it.'

'Well, anyway, I didn't notice. But my question went a bit further than the original charge, Antony. Are you thinking of something more than that?'

'My questions must have answered that for you. I'm thinking he may very well have killed Dobell himself.'

'If Moira Pershing took the dagger and we could find out that they met anywhere during the day – ' Peter broke off there. From where he was sitting he could see the street, and something had caught his attention. 'There's Sir Nicholas just coming in,' he said.

Antony twisted round in his chair so that he too could see what was happening beyond the window. An elderly Austin Princess was standing near the door of the hotel, and his uncle was just alighting from it. The years had probably done nothing to detract from the car's comfort, certainly nothing to impair its dignity. 'Where has he been, and where did he get hold of *that*?' said Antony in a hushed voice.

They weren't left long in doubt. Sir Nicholas might have seen them through the window, or he might have been led purely by instinct. In either event, he made straight for the bar on coming into the hotel. 'I thought I should find you here,' he said, coming to the table and pulling round a chair so that he could join them. In doing so he gave his nephew rather a piercing look, noted the signs of weariness, and said rather testily, 'You, I take it, have been busy.'

'I suppose we have.' For a moment the idea of conveying to his uncle the gist of their afternoon's activities seemed unbearable. 'I'll fill you in on everything, Uncle Nick, but not just now.'

'Later will do.' There was a pause, while he did his best to impress on the waitress his need for a really dry sherry. 'In any event, I should prefer Miss Langhorne to hear what you have to say as well.'

'But Miss Langhorne – '

'Is coming with us to London for the weekend. Jenny is expecting her.'

'That's good, of course, but – '

'Two reasons, Antony. First, I want her kept up to date on every aspect of the investigation. Secondly . . . has it occurred to you that she lives alone?'

'Oh, lord, no, I hadn't thought of that.'

'You mean, *she* might be attacked?' asked Peter incredulously.

'I mean exactly that. If you are right in your surmise, Antony, Mr. X might well take the line of least resistance and vent his spite on her . . . as a warning to you, shall we say?'

'I thought of that originally, when I didn't want to involve her at all and you said she'd be hurt if I didn't. But since I became so closely identified with the questions that are being asked . . . well – '

'You thought he would concentrate on you. I agree it seems most likely,' said Sir Nicholas, tart again. 'But we must not forget elementary precautions, for which reason I must ask you to exercise a certain amount of care yourself, Mr. Gibson, on your own behalf and on behalf of your family.'

'That's all very well, but I don't – '

'You are not yet convinced of your client's innocence.' Sir Nicholas rode smoothly over his objection.

'Are you?' asked Peter bluntly.

'I have sufficient doubts on the matter to feel that anyone

109

concerned in the investigation in any way should be careful
. . . very careful indeed.'

'In that case . . . we haven't any plans for this weekend,
so we'll all stay close to home. I don't expect we shall actually
have to withstand a siege,' said Peter, with a rather poor
attempt at humour.

Maitland had been thinking things out. 'No . . . look
here – ' he protested. 'I don't think any of us are in danger,
really I don't, Uncle Nick. Because if – if anything happened
it could be cited as proof of my theory . . . don't you think?'

'I still feel that Mr. Gibson should exercise caution, and
that I shall be happier if Miss Langhorne is with us in
Kempenfeldt Square.'

'That's where you've been,' said Antony, enlightened.
'Taking Vera home.'

'You surely did not think I should allow her to make use
of public transport when I had the time to accompany her.
She was kind enough to give me tea.'

'Then you saw her cottage. What did you think of it?'

'It wasn't the first time I had been there, if you remember.'

'No, of course, when Jeremy Skelton was on trial.'

'It's a charming place.' Sir Nicholas seemed quite content
with the change of subject, now that this warning had been
given. 'But small, very small.'

'For someone on their own – '

'I was thinking of the music she delights in so much. The
size of the room hardly does it justice.'

'That's right, of course.'

'I have been thinking, Antony, that the drawing-room in
Kempenfeldt Square is an ideal size and shape for adaptation
as a music room.'

'I suppose it is.' Maitland seemed puzzled by the suggestion. 'But, Uncle Nick, our room is splendid for music
too, and you always come upstairs when you feel like a
concert.'

'So I do.' There was a sort of blandness about Sir Nicholas
that his nephew couldn't quite make out. At this stage of an

investigation that he disapproved of he ought to have been cutting up rough; but apart from an occasional sharpness of tone he was amiability itself. 'I think we will dine in the Bar Mess tonight, Antony. That will give you a rest from Inspector Brady's affairs.'

XI

Maitland received the suggestion with gratitude, but through no fault of his own or his uncle's he wasn't to get away quite so easily. They had seen Peter Gibson on his way and Antony had just got into his own room when the phone rang and the desk clerk announced, in a tone vaguely apologetic, as though he knew the announcement would not be well received, 'Superintendent Harley is here to see you, Mr. Maitland.'

His first impulse was to say, 'Put him on,' and then to explain what shouldn't have needed explaining, 'I can't talk to you, you're a witness for the prosecution.' But then curiosity got the better of him, for surely Harley knew that already. Instead, 'I'll be right down,' he said.

Detective Superintendent Harley was waiting near the bottom of the stairs, as though he thought he must exercise some vigilance lest his quarry escape him. His face was surely intended by nature to have a good-humoured expression, but now he had a tight-lipped look. 'So you're Antony Maitland,' he said, without preamble. And then, abruptly, 'We'll go into the lounge.'

At this hour the lounge was deserted. Harley went as far as the middle of the room and then turned and said, still in the abrupt way that Maitland took to mean he had lost his temper irretrievably, 'You're interfering in what is purely a police matter.'

'Surely not, Superintendent. In the interests of my client –'

'The wrongful arrest case is as dead as mutton.'

'Do you think so? I should have said myself that one thing led to another.'

'I'm glad to hear you admit it. But you haven't been briefed to defend Brady on the murder charge.'

'I am, however, assisting in the preparation of the defence. And don't tell me it's unorthodox,' he added, when Harley seemed prepared with some angry retort. 'I'll *admit* that too, if you like. But there's absolutely nothing either you or anyone else can do to stop me.'

'These matters should be left to the police.'

'Is Dobell's murder still under investigation?'

'Not exactly.'

'I though not.'

'But – '

'R-routine matters connected with the p-prosecution. That isn't what I meant,' said Antony, who was beginning to lose his own temper.

'I don't understand you.'

'I mean that you c-can't say I'm obstructing the p-police.' He paused, making a real effort to overcome the stammer that always betrayed him in moments of anger. 'C-come off it, Superintendent, you haven't a leg to stand on, and we might as well bring this very pointless discussion to a close.'

'Very well, Mr. Maitland, very well.' The tight-lipped look was even more noticeable now. 'But I have one point to bring to your attention which even you, I think, will recognise as a legitimate complaint.'

'What is it?'

'You were given facilities to interview Inspector Brady at the police station – '

'That was a kindness I appreciated.'

' – but you had no earthly right to take Sergeant Cummings from his duties to answer your questions,' said Harley, ignoring the interruption.

'In the circumstances – '

'The circumstances are that the case for wrongful arrest is closed.'

'We've been through all that before.' Suddenly Antony was more tired than annoyed, but there was a question that must be asked. 'Have you been talking to John Irving?'

'N-no.'

'You don't sound very sure about that.'

'Of course I'm sure! I was merely making what seems a logical assumption.'

'I see. Well, Superintendent, in spite of what you say I must reserve the right to interview whom I choose in connection with Philip Brady's defence.'

'If you will not be warned, Mr. Maitland – '

'Warned?'

'That was the word I used.'

'Very well. I shall make sure I see Constable Peach at a time when he is not on duty. Will that content you?'

'If you propose to set the whole town by the ears with your questions – '

'It's no concern of yours.'

'Provided a breach of the peace is not committed. I have heard that once in Chedcombe – '

Antony was in no mood for reminiscences. 'It seems a somewhat unlikely contingency,' he said thoughtfully. 'Surely if someone makes an attack on me that fact would tend to suggest Philip Brady's innocence.'

'I don't follow your reasoning, I'm afraid. I can see you are not open to reason, Mr. Maitland, so I will say goodnight.'

Antony did not attempt to respond, but stood looking at the doorway through which the detective had disappeared for several seconds before he moved to follow. Harley had gone by the time he reached the hall; he went upstairs slowly, spent ten minutes in his own room, and then went along the corridor and knocked on his uncle's door. On being bidden to enter he did so, closed the door carefully and leaned back against it. 'I think before we go down to dinner, Uncle Nick, we'd better talk.'

Sir Nicholas was arranging his tie. He did not turn until

the job was finished but said, apparently addressing his reflection in the mirror, 'I told you, Antony, I should prefer Miss Langhorne to hear whatever you have to say.'

'I know you did, but this is important.' Sir Nicholas turned then and gave him the rather piercing look that he reserved for the occasions when he felt his nephew was not being quite frank with him. 'I needn't tell you the whole thing,' said Antony. 'Just enough to make you see – '

'Something has happened since we parted half an hour ago.'

'Superintendent Harley came to see me.'

'Surprising in the circumstances, but not, I should have thought, an earth-shattering event.'

'You see, Uncle Nick, I think he's Mr. X's go-between in Northdean.'

Sir Nicholas reached for his jacket and began to don it in his leisurely way. 'Now you do surprise me,' he said unemotionally. 'Have you any grounds for this belief, or is it one of your wilder guesses?'

'I'd better explain.' From his tone you would have thought the task was hopeless.

'It might be as well.' Sir Nicholas, apparently satisfied with his appearance, took the chintz-covered chair by the window, turned it slightly so that he could face his nephew where he still stood by the door.

'You see,' said Antony again, 'I set out to rattle the people I saw. What I did succeed in doing' – he smiled briefly at the memory – 'was rattle Peter Gibson, but that's beside the point.'

'Who were these witnesses?'

'John Irving. His wife calls him Johnny.'

'I cannot conceive that that piece of information is of the slightest use to either of us.'

'No, of course. What I was going to say . . . I believe, you know, that he *was* concerned in the diamond smuggling, and I let him see that very clearly. I also asked for his alibi for

Monday evening, which he declined to give me, though his wife, who is nervous, said he had been at home with her.'

'Was there anyone else whom you succeeded in making nervous during the course of the day?'

'Yes, Noyes, the barman here. What I was after, Uncle Nick, was some reaction from the next chap in line above them, the one who gave them their orders.'

'And you think that Superintendent Harley's visit was such a reaction?'

'It was sheer nonsense. He was angry, so angry he had to say something, whether it made sense or not. He was trying to accuse me of obstructing the police in the course of their duty, and when I didn't buy that' – Sir Nicholas closed his eyes for a moment, as if in pain – 'he actually brought up the fact that we'd talked to Sergeant Cummings at a time when he was officially on duty.'

'Let me ask you one question, Antony. What reaction did you expect to get from the – shall we say, the intermediary?'

'I didn't much care.'

'Well, I care,' said Sir Nicholas very gently. 'I do not know, you see, how long my reputation can stand the strain of constant association with you. And I imagine Jenny might care, for reasons of her own, if the reaction you speak of had taken the form of an attack on you.'

Maitland left the door and took a quick turn about the room, coming to a halt again at the foot of the bed. 'But I told you, Uncle Nick, I don't think that's going to happen. Anything that could be used in Brady's favour – '

'You forget your reputation, my dear boy. Your unfortunate reputation for meddling. In your case I am afraid it could be plausibly suggested that someone out of the past – '

That brought Antony up short. It also annoyed him. 'The reaction was s-surely h-harmless enough,' he said at length, carefully; but his uncle heard and recognised the slight, angry stammer and his own voice grew cold.

'You have yet to convince me – '

'Believe me, Uncle N-nick, he'd not h-have c-come to me with such a s-stupid complaint unless he was badly w-worried by what you call my m-meddling.'

'Nothing will be gained by losing your temper, Antony,' Sir Nicholas pointed out. At which Maitland suddenly threw caution to the winds, threw up his hands and said despairingly,

'Oh, what's the use!'

That brought about an immediate change of mood on the older man's part. 'If it will make you any happier we will admit the truth of what you say, for the sake of argument. What is so worrying about it? If you really believe you have identified one of your villains you should be pleased about it, or so I should have thought.'

Antony went again to the window and back. 'If I thought I could prove it,' he said. 'But what earthly chance have we if the investigating officer is himself guilty of the crime our client is accused of? And Brady's position – '

'Is no worse than it was before.'

'I suppose not. But there ought to be something we could do.'

'Allow me some time to think about the matter. In the meantime, if we intend to follow my suggestion about dining in the Bar Mess it is high time we went down. It would not be courteous,' he went on, getting to his feet and making his way unhurriedly towards the door, 'to arrive after the soup is on the table.'

Antony recognised only too well something inexorable in his uncle's tone. 'The thing is,' he said, 'what will Mr. X do next?'

'That, my dear boy,' said Sir Nicholas, holding the door open invitingly, 'we shall just have to wait and see.'

XII

So they went down to join their fellow members of the

Bar Mess, among whom was Wellesley, obviously chock-full of curiosity but refraining with real nobility from open questioning. Sir Nicholas gave every evidence of enjoying his evening, but Antony was inclined to be thoughtful and excused himself early so that he could have a longish chat with Jenny. That was comforting: if she guessed Sir Nicholas's purpose in inviting Vera Langhorne for the week-end she said nothing of it; nothing either of any worries she might be entertaining on her husband's behalf. But his shoulder was aching too much by the time he got to bed to allow him to sleep deeply, and he spent a restless night.

THURSDAY, 27th MAY

I

'What are your plans for this morning, Antony?' enquired Sir Nicholas, when they met for breakfast the following day. His tone was perhaps over casual, as though he detected in his nephew a tendency to nervousness that he had no desire to encourage.

'If I can see Constable Peach, if he isn't on duty, I shall do that, though I can't imagine he'll have anything to tell me beyond corroborating what Brady has had to say about the case against Dobell and Irving. There's also Harold Hargreaves, their employer, about whom I know nothing except that he's old-fashioned and doesn't approve of over-time . . . if he has to pay for it, I suppose. Before Harley came here yesterday evening I'd toyed with the idea that Hargreaves might be a go-between, but now I'm not so interested in him.'

'A more mature reflection has not caused you to revise your opinion then?'

'Did you think it might have?'

'I wondered.' Sir Nicholas helped himself to another piece of toast. 'Well, it doesn't sound as if either of us will be busy. I am sending the car for Miss Langhorne, she will be joining us for luncheon, and if you do not require my presence I shall probably go to Chedcombe myself, as she seems to have some scruples about the extravagance of riding alone. That will give us time to catch the train at leisure, will it not?'

'It will.' There could be no doubt that Maitland's attention was not altogether on what his uncle was saying. He might almost have been expecting that their meal would be interrupted; at any rate, when Peter Gibson appeared in the doorway he was the first to see him and raise his hand to signal their position. They were at a table for four, so there was room for the solicitor to join them. (Antony himself had often been relegated to one of the small tables near the wall, but he doubted whether Sir Nicholas, even when alone, had ever been placed in such cramped circumstances.) Peter gave them the barest 'Good morning' as he seated himself, looked from one of them to the other for a moment as though trying to assess in advance the effect of what he was going to say, and then stated baldly,

'Something's happened. I don't know whether it will interest you or not. Superintendent Harley is dead.'

That brought a second or two of absolute stillness on Antony's part. Then he said, his eyes fixed with a rather embarrassing intentness on Peter's face, 'I'm interested all right. How did he die?'

'He had an accident on his way home last night.'

'Tell me about it. And, as a matter of interest, how did you hear? It can't be in the papers yet.'

'I phoned the police station this morning to get Peach's address and find out whether he'd be at work or at home this morning. I was put through to Inspector Mawson and he told me.'

'What exactly – ?'

'Harley was late going home. He lives about ten miles out on the Chedcombe road. There's a quarry off to the left, about two miles this side of his house. He'd gone through the railings and crashed over. That's how he was found; someone who knew the road and knew it was a fresh break went to inspect and saw the car. It hadn't burned, but he hadn't a chance, of course. It's quite fifty feet to the bottom.'

'I see. I had a visit from the Superintendent after you left us yesterday, Peter. I'd better tell you what he had to say, and the conclusion I reached.'

Gibson listened in silence. As the recital finished his eyes

119

were on Sir Nicholas. 'What do *you* think about that?' he asked.

Sir Nicholas smiled. 'Yesterday evening, I must admit, my feelings were about as sceptical as I see yours are now. But in view of what you tell us – '

'It's perfectly obvious.' Maitland was impatient. 'I said I wondered what Mr. X's next move would be, and this is it. He's cutting his losses.'

'But Harley's death was an accident.'

'Don't be naive, Peter. It may look that way, but I'll bet you anything you like Mr. X was behind it. This way there's no link between him and any of the people in Northdean. Which doesn't simplify matters from our point of view.'

'You're forgetting one thing, Antony,' Sir Nicholas put in. And added, when his nephew looked at him enquiringly, 'Miss Moira Pershing.'

'Yes, I was forgetting her. But we don't know really whether she knows Mr. X, or whether she was recruited by Harley. I'd guess at the latter, myself.'

'Do you really believe that the Superintendent – ?' Peter didn't try to complete the query, but his incredulity was obvious.

'I do. Uncle Nick, you believe me *now*, don't you?'

'To make use of one of your own turns of phrase, Antony, the odds against this fatality being a coincidence seem to be astronomical.'

'All right then.' It wasn't clear whether Peter was really convinced, or whether he just didn't care to contradict so formidable a personage as Sir Nicholas. 'If it was murder, where does that leave us?'

'It complicates the situation, certainly.' Sir Nicholas was decisive. 'I think the first thing we must do, Antony, is to see the Chief Constable. He can put in train the necessary enquiries into the whereabouts and safety of Miss Pershing.'

'Whoever is in charge of the detective branch – ' said Antony, but his uncle interrupted him, saying firmly,

'Will be for the moment someone in a quite junior capacity. In any event, the Chief Constable is the one we must see. This is a case for Scotland Yard, and that must be a matter for his decision.'

'All right then.' He did not feel inclined to argue, though he foresaw difficulties ahead. It would serve no useful purpose. 'Who is the Chief Constable, Peter? And where does he live?'

II

They separated an hour later, and already by that time several things had been accomplished. Antony had given his uncle a condensed account of his activities the previous day (Sir Nicholas had a sour look for some of them, but made no comment); Peter Gibson, not without some misgivings, had telephoned Colonel Wycherley, the Chief Constable, and obtained his agreement to the proposed interview; and Sir Nicholas had arranged for the Austin Princess to convey Miss Vera Langhorne in a suitably dignified fashion from Chedcombe.

The meeting was to take place at the police station, which presented to their eyes when they arrived a scene of some confusion. Perhaps that was not surprising in view of the death of the chief of the detective branch and the incarceration of his lieutenant. Colonel Wycherley had taken possession, for the time being, of Superintendent Harley's office, and contrived to make himself look very much at home there. He was a dapper little man, one of the older breed of Chief Constables who had been appointed from outside the force, but he had a natural air of authority and, to Antony's mind at least, the post fitted him like a glove.

'Everything at sixes and sevens this morning,' he told them, after the first greetings had been exchanged. 'You've heard – I'd be surprised in a place like Northdean if you hadn't heard – of the dreadful thing that happened to poor Harley?'

'In a sense,' said Sir Nicholas, 'that is why we are here.' Maitland was happy enough to let his uncle take the initiative, being firmly convinced that it was Sir Nicholas's name alone that had persuaded Wycherley to see them. 'We were told there had been an accident. I suppose there is no question in your mind about that.'

That brought a sudden frown and a lowering glance in Maitland's direction. 'The man is certainly dead,' said the Chief Constable dryly. 'I haven't a detailed report yet, but there seems no doubt that he met his death as a result of multiple injuries sustained in an accident. Are you suggesting anything else?'

'There is some reason to believe that the accident was . . . contrived.'

'Indeed?' A definitely chilly note was creeping into the proceedings and Antony, reprehensibly perhaps, found himself a prey to amusement. For the first time in his life it occurred to him as a possibility that some day his uncle might meet his match. 'I must ask you to explain that, Sir Nicholas,' Wycherley went on.

'That, after all,' said Sir Nicholas imperturbably, 'is what I am here for. You may know that I am representing Philip Brady, one of your officers, in the murder charge that has been brought against him, and that my nephew, at my request, is assisting in the preparation of the defence.' (Well, that version had the advantage of sounding better than an account of the behind-the-scenes in-fighting that had actually taken place.)

'I have heard of Mr. Maitland.' The dry note was still there.

'You will remember, too, the Barnard case, which also had a background of diamond smuggling.' Sir Nicholas was well launched now, and it was doubtful whether he noticed anything amiss in the atmosphere. 'In the course of that enquiry he met a man whose name he did not and does not know, but who was very evidently the – er – the master-mind behind the whole business. It pains me to borrow terms from sensational fiction, but nothing else will serve. I am sure you will agree that it was natural, when he was called in again, in the same town, in a case that involved diamond smuggling, that his mind should turn to this man, whom I am constrained to refer to as Mr. X.'

'I have heard of Mr. Maitland,' said Wycherley again. 'There is nothing to surprise me in the circumstances you have outlined.'

'As you know, it was originally the wrongful arrest accusation that interested him. In the course of investigating that, and in view of the murder of one of the plaintiffs, he has come to certain conclusions. With which, I may say, I have been brought to concur. I am afraid it is rather a lengthy story, but I shall be grateful if you will listen to it.'

The Chief Constable looked at him more in sorrow than in anger now. 'If there is any doubt at all about the cause of poor Harley's death,' he said, 'I should of course wish to know it. But I cannot believe that, you know. It is getting into the realm of melodrama.'

'I have often felt the same way myself,' said Sir Nicholas cordially. Maitland, on whom the effect of being talked of as if he wasn't there was to make him feel like the invisible man, cleared his throat unnecessarily. 'I am sure you will be as concise as you can,' said his uncle in an encouraging way.

He should have needed no encouragement; the matter was close enough to his heart, and filled his mind almost to the exclusion of everything else. But he set out to be deliberately matter-of-fact. If there was melodrama in the situation, as Wycherley had pointed out, he wasn't going to emphasise it. 'I'd better begin at the beginning,' he said, 'with my meeting with Mr. X. Then you'll be able to see why I connected him

123

immediately with the new bout of diamond smuggling in Northdean. This is how it was . . .'

This morning Sir Nicholas was on his best behaviour and listened to the recital without comment. It couldn't be said that the Chief Constable was a bad listener either, unless his frowning look was to be regarded as a comment in itself, but he was moved to expostulation when Maitland came to the end of his account of his talk with Mr. X. 'And that was six years ago, or very nearly, and you have done nothing to see that this man was apprehended.'

Sir Nicholas took fire at that. 'In the circumstances that have been described to you . . . a visit paid to an unknown man, in an unknown place, at gun point – '

Antony, however, had no intention of apologising for the episode. 'I made a bargain with the man,' he said. (Sir Nicholas later insisted that this was a piece of pure provocation; his nephew's denials did not seem to impress him at all.)

'With someone you knew to be a criminal.' Wycherley's tone was accusing.

'You must remember that I had no proof of that, except what he himself told me. Easily enough denied at a later date. But beyond anything else I did not know who he was, and as he was obviously a dangerous person to tangle with I had no real incentive to find out. Now, however – '

'Yes, there seems to have been a change in your attitude. According to your own admission – '

'Now, there's a word I hate,' Maitland told him. 'However, I will admit, if you like, that I now think it's time the man was stopped. I don't know if my description of our talk conveyed to you that he has a strong streak of megalomania. Now I'd say at a guess that side of his character is taking over to an even greater extent. If he's thinking of murder as the answer to every question that arises – '

'You have yet to convince me of that.' Whether out of curiosity as to what the next point would be, or from a more reasoned decision that his complaints weren't likely to get him anywhere, Colonel Wycherley had decided to leave a contentious topic.

'Very well. I believe the course of events to have been as follows: Dobell and Irving were guilty as charged, but their acquittal was arranged by the suborning of witnesses, whether by bribery or threats, or by a mixture of both I don't know. Philip Brady, however, did not intend to let the matter rest there. Even without the information I had at my disposal he came to the conclusion that somebody stood behind the two defendants, and he intended to continue his enquiries until he found out who it was. This decision was, I understand, generally known among his colleagues. To distract his attention the case for wrongful arrest was brought and the matter might have ended there if I had not been brought into the affair. You have said, Colonel, that you have heard of me; I take it that you mean you know I have a reputation for what my uncle is pleased to call meddling. Remember then that Mr. X had actually met me, and knew very well who I was. A rather drastic decision was then taken: to murder Dobell – whom we must assume to have been the weaker link in the chain – and provide such strong evidence against Brady that I should lose interest in any investigation I might have had in mind. This was a good plan, and might have had exactly the desired effect, if it had not been for the fact that I believed my client when he protested his innocence.'

'You were, however, basing your belief on instinct rather than on evidence.' The Chief Constable sounded thoughtful now, as though against his will he saw some force in Maitland's arguments.

'I'm afraid that's true. But if Brady was not guilty of framing the charge against Dobell and Irving . . . and I think even you, Colonel, will admit that it was unlikely.'

'I didn't think he would have been quite so foolish,' Wycherley admitted. 'But the evidence against him on the more serious charge – '

'If you could believe in threats, intimidation, what you will, in the first case, why not in the second?'

'You really believe what you are telling me, don't you?' The Chief Constable's tone was wondering, and suddenly Maitland laughed and, looking round, surprised an answering smile on Sir Nicholas's face.

'Do you think I'd have been rash enough to come here if I didn't? I assure you – ' He broke off there because, to his astonishment. Wycherley was laughing too. 'It isn't funny,' he said then, unfairly, but sounded only mildly protesting. 'If I can't convince you – '

'Sincerity is unmistakable. I have also to bear in mind that Sir Nicholas has given your cause his blessing, and I am sure he is not one of the most credulous of men.'

'It was what happened this morning that convinced him,' said Antony. 'But I'm getting ahead of my story. The rest is easily told. I was persuaded – need I go into my reasons? – that Mr. X wasn't known to the rank and file of his organisation, or to the people who were persuaded to perjure themselves in defence of Dobell and Irving. In short, that there was a go-between who took care of all these matters for him.'

'That seems a reasonable supposition,' nodded the Chief Constable, which distracted Antony for a moment, until he realised that it reminded him of one of the judge's remarks in *Trial by Jury*. 'There is, however, the question – '

'I wondered when you'd think of that. You have only my word for Mr. X's existence.'

'Sir Nicholas – '

'Even he doesn't *know*. He was aware of the fruits of my conference with the gentleman, however, which is in itself a kind of proof.'

'I am not doubting your veracity, Mr. Maitland, only – perhaps – the conclusions you draw in this particular case.'

'You won't accept the go-between?'

'I said it seemed reasonable to take his existence for granted. Let us go on from there.'

'Very well. I set out yesterday morning with the deliberate intention of scaring two of the witnesses I believed to have perjured themselves . . . John Irving and Noyes, the barman. With Noyes I think I succeeded; Irving is a cooler customer, but his wife was nervous. I wouldn't mind betting she worked on him after I'd gone.'

'And the purpose of this . . . would intimidation be too strong a word, Mr. Maitland?'

'I made no threats.' Antony seemed to be taking the question seriously. 'I thought they'd appeal to the next man up, the go-between, and then I hoped for some reaction from him.'

'It didn't occur to you that the reaction might take the form of an attack on yourself?'

'As a matter of fact, no. It occurred to my uncle, however. He said . . . well, that's not strictly relevant. But I did get my reaction, Colonel. Later that same evening Superintendent Harley came to see me.'

That brought another of those moments of complete silence. Antony looked, as he had sounded, casual enough, but in fact he was alert for his audience's reaction. And Wycherley was not in any hurry to speak, he might almost have been spinning out the tension deliberately. When he did speak he had gone back to the colder tone with which he had received the beginning of the story. 'I think you had better tell me exactly what you mean by that, Mr. Maitland.'

'He came to me with a ridiculous complaint, something about obstructing the police, that wouldn't hold water for an instant. When I pointed that out to him he changed his tack and expressed his surprise and resentment that I had presumed to question Sergeant Cummings while he was officially on duty. I suppose the last point was valid enough, though it hardly seemed sufficient to warrant the anger he displayed. This was quite out of all proportion to any reason he could have had for disliking my activities. I therefore, assumed, not unnaturally, I think, that this was the reaction I was looking for . . . that Superintendent Harley was, in fact, the go-between.'

'You're telling me that one of my own men – '

'Before you go any further, Colonel, may I point out that Philip Brady is also one of your own men.'

'But I've known Harley for years! '

'If you're doubting my conclusions again, I think I should also point out that I expressed this opinion to my uncle last night. He was then inclined to doubt me, but when we heard of Harley's death – ' He didn't try to finish that and again there was a silence until the Chief Constable said distressfully.

'Yes, I see. This is a terrible thing you are telling me. Sir Nicholas – '

'I don't like coincidences,' said Sir Nicholas flatly.

'Of course not, but . . . are you quite sure, Mr. Maitland, that there can be no other explanation?'

'I've been warned off the grass before,' said Antony, 'but not quite in that way. In fact – I think I should have remembered it perhaps when you were castigating me for my lack of action – one such case was when Chief Inspector Sykes tried to discourage me from looking into the matter of diamond smuggling in the first place. But that was out of concern for my safety, not for any other reason.'

'And now you're telling me that Harley was murdered.'

'I don't like coincidences,' said Antony, as his uncle had done.

'But . . . in heaven's name, why?'

'To sever any link between what has been happening locally and Mr. X.'

'In that event . . . Sir Nicholas, I appeal to you. What should I do?'

Sir Nicholas smiled. 'It goes against the grain for me to say so, but I think you should listen to my nephew.'

'I have listened!' said Wycherley in an overwrought way.

'Then you can tell me at least, has he raised no doubts in your mind?'

'Of course he has raised doubts. I – '

'Then I think . . . I take it your own Criminal Investigation Department has been depleted by recent events.'

'Depleted? It's practically non-existent!'

'Then it seems to me – I am sure upon reflection you will come to the same conclusion – that it is a matter for Scotland Yard. At least they will set your mind at rest as to whether a murder – a second murder, I should say – has been committed.'

'You're right, of course.' This was said with something like a groan. 'There is also the question of whether Harley is guilty as you say, Mr. Maitland. I should know the answer to that for my own satisfaction; though I suppose dissatisfaction would be a better term.'

'Come now,' said Antony in a pleased tone, 'that sounds as if you were beginning to believe me.'

'If I must be frank with you,' said Wycherley unhappily, 'every instinct tells me you're wrong . . . I know Harley, you see. On the other hand – ' But it was too difficult. The sentence was never completed.

'You do see – don't you? – that something has got to be done about Philip Brady.'

'In face of the evidence – '

'Yes. I know all about that. I'm only saying that Dobell's murder too is a proper field for Scotland Yard's investigations.'

'I realise that.'

'Then we needn't keep you any longer. Unless . . . you've something else on your mind, Uncle Nick.'

'I was thinking, Colonel, if you will forgive a further suggestion, that perhaps you might be able to request the services of Chief Inspector Sykes, who was the first person to put my nephew to some degree in the picture as regards diamond smuggling into and out of this country.'

'I shall certainly endeavour to do so.' He paused, looking from one of them to the other. 'Mr. Maitland, what are your immediate plans?'

'I was going back to town, but obviously I must stay here until Sykes – or whoever it is – arrives . . . don't you think?'

'That was in my mind. It is a relief to know that you agree with me.'

Maitland was already on his feet, and the Chief Constable was following his example, when Sir Nicholas came back into the conversation again. 'There is one thing we are forgetting, Antony. The question of Miss Pershing.'

'That's right. You see, Colonel, if she's telling lies as I believe someone prevailed on her to do, it might have been Harley, it might have been Mr. X himself, and if the latter then we think she is in danger too. I can't approach her in the circumstances, but do you think one of your men – ?'

'That is a good point, I shall attend to it. Believe me, gentlemen, I appreciate your confiding in me.'

Sir Nicholas came to his feet too. 'There was really nothing else to be done,' he pointed out. And began, with the touch of formality that some people relished while others found it affected, to make his farewells.

III

'Do you think he finally believed us, Uncle Nick?' asked Maitland as they reached the street again. 'He was polite enough, but with a chap like him it's difficult to tell.'

'He believed us.' Sir Nicholas was positive. 'He saw the force of your arguments. He also appreciated the fact that you are sincere in what you say.'

'But still there was an unwillingness.'

'Very naturally. Superintendent Harley is an institution

in the town, very well thought of, from what your friend Gibson told you.'

'He is also said, by popular report, to have a rich wife. Wycherley may remember that when he thinks things over. But to get back to Harley's reputation, I suppose Mr. X just couldn't resist the idea of recruiting a chap like that.' There was a silence before he spoke again. 'I've got to stay on, Uncle Nick, though I'll try to get home tomorrow night or Saturday morning. What about you?'

'I am not quite sure.'

'If we're right about the motive behind Harley's death – '

'You are trying to tell me you are no longer in danger. If I must be honest with you, Antony, my position is very like the one in which the Chief Constable finds himself. My mind accepts the fact, but still I am uneasy.'

'Don't be. I know what you said when you arrived, but you really can't hang about here doing nothing.'

'Very well then. Miss Langhorne and I will take the afternoon train as planned. Jenny will be glad of the company in your absence,' he added, in the sort of voice that he might have used to forestall a protest. But Antony was thinking about Moira Pershing, and wondering just where she fitted into the picture, and for once he did not even think of arguing with Sir Nicholas's stated intention.

IV

Vera Langhorne arrived in time for lunch, but Sir Nicholas forbade shop talk and the meal passed pleasantly enough. For want of anything better to do Antony saw them off that afternoon at the station, and because he had grave doubts as to what they would find to talk about, purchased a number of magazines to while away the tedium of the journey.

He needn't have worried. 'I don't know what he was

thinking of,' said Sir Nicholas testily, disposing of the pile neatly on an empty seat. 'All this rubbish. Unless – ?'

'Rather talk,' Vera assured him with one of her rather grim smiles. 'Said you wanted me kept in the picture.'

'Indeed I do. And as we are alone in the carriage this seems an excellent opportunity to bring you up to date. I must also apologise for not coming in person to fetch you this morning.'

'Not necessary.'

'It would have been a pleasure. But as things turned out . . . you have heard, perhaps, of Superintendent Harley's death.'

'Driver told me. Something of a sensation,' said Vera with her usual economy of words.

'I must first explain to you something of the tactics that Antony employed yesterday . . .' When he wanted to, Sir Nicholas could be almost as succinct as his companion. The tale, therefore, was quickly and clearly told. He concluded by saying, 'I have put the idea into Colonel Wycherley's head that Chief Inspector Sykes would be an excellent choice to investigate these matters. Antony should thank me for that.'

'He's determined to continue his own enquiries?'

'More determined than ever, though I do not think there is much he can do in Northdean at the moment. He says Mr. X has washed his hands of the operation there, and that therefore there is no further danger to anybody.'

Miss Langhorne considered that before replying. 'Inclined to agree with him,' she said at length. 'Only thing is, if he gets too close – '

'I am consoling myself with the reflection that that will be difficult to do.'

'Surely if there's to be a police investigation of the part Superintendent Harley played in the affair, that should suffice to clear Philip Brady. Main thing, after all.'

'You would think so.' Sir Nicholas's agreement was

cordial. 'However, Antony seems to have decided that Mr. X is a megalomaniac. I think I can quote his own words on the subject. "If he's thinking of murder as the answer to every question that arises, something has got to be done about him." '

'See his point, but not his job,' said Vera firmly.

'I wish you might have more success than I in convincing him of that. He's got some idea in his head – ' He broke off there, without attempting to finish the sentence.

'What sort of idea?' asked Vera, when she was sure she wouldn't be interrupting him.

'He won't tell me. And that's reasonable, I suppose,' said Sir Nicholas with uncharacteristic frankness. 'He knows well enough that I should try to discourage him.'

'When is he coming back to town?'

'Tomorrow afternoon, or perhaps Saturday morning. After he has seen Chief Inspector Sykes, in any case.'

'What sort of a man is he?'

'Sykes? Sensible sort of fellow,' said Sir Nicholas vaguely.

'You said Antony should thank you for suggesting his name to the Chief Constable.'

'He finds Sykes easier to work with than some others I could mention. I suppose it's not unnatural that Scotland Yard should regard his activities with a somewhat dubious eye.'

'Seems unnatural to me. Always on the side of justice,' said Vera, rather severely.

'There have been occasions . . . but that, my dear Miss Langhorne, is going a long way back into the past.'

'Like to hear. So long as you want to tell me, of course,' she added scrupulously.

They were approaching the terminus when Sir Nicholas glanced out of the window and stopped in mid-sentence. 'You must forgive me for having run on so, Miss Langhorne. I had no idea how long I had been talking.'

'See why you're worried,' said Vera thoughtfully.

133

Sir Nicholas smiled at her, suddenly and brilliantly. He was conscious of a quite extraordinary feeling of release, something that a more impetuous man, one who was given to confiding his feelings to others, might experience three times a week, but that was quite foreign to him. 'When we have quarrelled most bitterly,' he said, 'Antony has reminded me that he is only following my precepts. I suppose I should be grateful that he has so much proper feeling.'

'Think you should,' said Vera, returning his smile. 'But you know,' she added, 'going back to Mr. X and his affairs, doesn't seem much point after all in my coming to London with you.'

'I explained to you – ' For the second time, Sir Nicholas did not attempt to complete what he was saying.

'Some nonsense about my advice. You don't need it,' said Vera, 'and wouldn't take it if I offered it to you.'

'I assure you – ' began Sir Nicholas, and for the first time in their acquaintance became aware that she was laughing at him. 'Well, I admit,' he concluded weakly, 'I had some fears for your safety, living alone as you do. And when it seemed those fears were no longer valid it seemed a shame to disturb such a pleasant arrangement. Have I offended you?'

'Not in the least.'

'Besides, Jenny will be glad of the company.'

Miss Langhorne had a grunt for that, which might have been construed as indicating disbelief. But as the train was already pulling into the platform at Paddington Station, no more was said.

V

Antony, meantime, was at a loose end. He went straight from the station to Peter Gibson's office, where he was regaled with tea and Marie biscuits, and brought the solicitor up to date on the outcome of the interview with the Chief Constable. 'Do you think he believed you?' asked Peter when he had finished.

'Uncle Nick says he did, I can't make up my mind. Anyway, the results couldn't have been better; he agreed to ask Scotland Yard's help . . . preferably in the person of Chief Inspector Sykes.'

'Why – ?'

'Because he's the only one there I'm more or less on friendly terms with. As a matter of fact, I don't think he always altogether trusts me . . . when I'm acting on a hunch he thinks I *know* something that I'm keeping to myself. But he has a strict sense of fairness and always pays his debts.'

'What do you mean?'

'He seems to think I've done a favour or two for him in the past. That means, you see, that whether he altogether believes me or not, at least the question of Superintendent Harley's involvement in Mr. X's affairs will be thoroughly gone into . . . including, of course, the framing of Philip Brady. That ought to result in his being cleared . . . don't you think?'

'I've been doing a good deal of thinking since this morning,' Peter told him.

'With what result?'

'I've come to the conclusion . . . well, if Sir Nicholas believes you about Dobell's murder, who am I to doubt you?'

Antony grinned. 'I could have wished you'd been convinced by the force of my arguments, but still – '

'The trouble is, I'm not so certain as you seem to be that the evidence against Philip can be proved to be false.'

'Wait a bit! Do you mean by that that you still think he's guilty?'

'No. I said I'd come round to your way of thinking. I meant just what I said.'

'And you're right, of course. There's no guarantee Sykes

will be able to clear him. Only I don't see what else I can do until he's had a shot at it, do you?'

'Does that mean you're giving up the case altogether?'

'Not a bit of it. I shall approach it from the other end, that's all.'

'Through Mr. X?'

'That's right. I meant what I said this morning, Peter, it's time something was done about him.'

'But I don't see how you can prove anything.'

'I've a great faith in the police, especially if you can point them in the right direction. All the same – '

'You're not really so sure you can find him,' said Gibson shrewdly.

'Of course I'm not sure!' If he had been trying for a complacent note, those few words betrayed his real feelings. There was a pause, and then he pushed his cup across the desk. 'Is there any more tea in that pot, Peter? Because if there is, I'd be glad of it.'

VI

He dined with the Gibsons that evening, and felt the better for it. Peter had promised 'no shop', and except for an occasional lamentation from Lucy about their friend Philip's uncomfortable circumstances, this was faithfully adhered to. Lucy had heard of Superintendent Harley's death and was inclined to lament that too, but, of course, she knew nothing of the suggestion that Antony had put forward, and neither her husband nor their guest attempted to enlighten her.

When he got back to the hotel there was a message to ring Chief Inspector Sykes however late he got in. It was only half-past ten, so he would in any case have had no scruples about doing this. He went up to his room and picked up the telephone.

The number he had been given turned out to be that of

a hostelry called the Blue Boar, which he vaguely remembered noticing on some of his travels around the town. He was quickly put through to Sykes's room and said, as soon as the detective's sense of propriety was satisfied and he had been assured of Jenny's health and Sir Nicholas's well-being, 'I'm glad you were able to come.'

Sykes had never lost his north-country accent, and now there was as well some amusement in his tone. 'Now, as I understand it, I didn't have much choice, and it was something Sir Nicholas said to Colonel Wycherley – '

'He suggested your name, certainly, but I wasn't sure you would be free.'

'When the Assistant Commissioner heard you were mixed up in the matter somehow – ' said Sykes, and again was interrupted.

'Have you seen Wycherley?' Maitland demanded.

'I have.'

'And did he tell you my ideas about all this?'

'He briefed me very thoroughly.'

'Then, what do you think?'

'Nay, Mr. Maitland, it's early days yet,' Sykes protested. 'But – '

'I have put enquiries in train. You know these things can't be hurried. I'll want to see you, of course.'

'That's why I'm still here. When? Now?'

'Tomorrow,' said Sykes firmly. 'Tomorrow afternoon will be time enough. I've got things to take care of in the morning. Will that suit you, Mr. Maitland?'

'I suppose it must.' It wasn't easy for him to repress his eagerness. 'Look here, Chief Inspector, you won't forget Philip Brady is in prison awaiting trial, will you? For a crime I'm sure he didn't commit.'

'I'm not likely to be allowed to forget it.' The amusement was clearly to be heard in Sykes's voice again. 'And now may I ask you a question, Mr. Maitland? Do you remember Roy Bromley?'

'Roy – ? Good lord, that was years ago. Of course I remember him, but the cases weren't in any way parallel.'

'He wasn't quite as innocent as you thought,' said Sykes gently. And then, 'Good night, Mr. Maitland, I'll be with you at two o'clock tomorrow.'

'Where? Here?'

'If you mean the Red Lion, yes. It seems as convenient a place as any.'

'I thought you might be staying here yourself.'

'No room. Too many of your professional brethren in town. Tomorrow, Mr. Maitland,' said Sykes again. 'At two o'clock.' This time he replaced the receiver without waiting for any further comment.

So there was nothing left to do before turning in but to phone Jenny. He could hear music in the background when she answered, one of their Vaughan Williams records that was fairly new, so probably Vera hadn't heard it before. 'They got home safely then?' he asked.

'I'd hoped you'd be with them; but, yes, they got home quite safely.'

'I could get the late train tomorrow . . . home about midnight, love. Sykes doesn't want to see me until the afternoon, and from something he said he doesn't seem particularly receptive to my ideas, so I don't see any way of getting through with it quickly.'

'Uncle Nick told me – '

'Then you understand why I couldn't come. Jenny, will you phone Roger tomorrow – '

'He was here this evening. He only just left.'

' – and make sure I see him during the weekend . . . Saturday for choice. Meg too, of course, but it's Roger I want to talk to.'

'I'll tell him.' Some of the brightness seemed to have gone out of her voice and he hastened to reassure her.

'Don't worry, love. Sykes will take care of everything.'

'I'm not,' she told him. And then, because that was a lie

and both of them knew it (though perhaps no more of a lie than the implication of his statement to her had been), she changed the subject without too much finesse. 'Roger says Meg's play will be coming off in a week or two.'

'Is he glad?'

'He didn't say so, but I think he hopes she'll rest this summer. It would be nice for him to see a little bit more of her.'

'Let's hope another part doesn't come along too quickly then.' They talked in a determined way about their friends for another few minutes, and rang off at last, each of them with a vaguely dissatisfied feeling.

FRIDAY, 28th MAY

I

The morning passed slowly, he was unable to settle to a book, and though he tried to do some constructive thinking this didn't get him very far. Maitland lunched early and sat over the meal as long as he decently could, but by the time Sykes arrived at the hotel he was in a state of seething impatience.

Detective Chief Inspector Sykes was a square-built, fresh-faced man, who always put Antony in mind of a farmer on market day . . . a farmer, perhaps, who had just put through a good deal. Maitland went down to the hall to greet him, and led the way back to his room. 'At least we can be private here, if not very comfortable,' he said. 'Wouldn't it have been better to meet at the police station?'

'After what you've been saying about some of the things that go on in Northdean,' said Sykes, seating himself without protest in the one armchair, 'I should have thought it would be the last place in the world for a private conference.'

'But Harley's dead.'

'So he is. Now, what have you to tell me about that, Mr. Maitland?'

Antony temporised. He wasn't quite sure what instinct made him do this, after all to talk to Sykes was what he had stayed over for, but suddenly he was unwilling to launch yet again into his story. 'Hasn't Colonel Wycherley told you?' he said.

'I believe he filled me in very well. But now, if you don't mind – '

'First, what do you think of my ideas?'

Sykes took his time over that. 'Would it be too unkind to say they seem a little far-fetched?' he said at last.

And that, after all, was what he had feared. 'I convinced Uncle Nick,' he said.

'I can see how that happened. The fact that you spoke to him one evening about Harley, and wondered what your Mr. X was going to do next, and the next morning heard that the Superintendent had been found dead – '

'Do you like coincidences, Chief Inspector?'

'No more than you do. Until we have some certain indication that the death was not purely accidental, however, I should prefer to reserve judgment.'

'I see. What are you doing about that?'

'I am awaiting the pathologist's report. Sir Richard Pontefract . . . I imagine even you will accept his findings.'

'There would still remain the question of Mr. X. And someone in Northdean – not Philip Brady – killed Dobell and persuaded a number of people to give false evidence.'

'Obviously, Mr. Maitland,' – this was a complaint that Sykes had made many times before – 'you know something that I do not.'

'Only, for sure, that Mr. X exists.' And that was as good a place as any to begin his tale. 'You remember the Barnard case?'

'Very well. You disregarded my warning, Mr. Maitland, from what the Chief Constable tells me.'

'It was something that had to be done.'

'Perhaps. But don't you think that, having come into contact with this man, you might have given me a hint?'

'What about? I didn't know who he was, or where he lived. The fact that he existed – that someone existed who was organising the whole business – you knew for yourself.'

'So I did.' Sykes smiled in his sedate way. 'Well, I see I must absolve you from any blame on that score . . . as Colonel

Wycherley seems to have done. Tell me about your meeting with this Mr. X of yours. I won't interrupt again.'

So Maitland talked and Sykes listened, as he had promised, in silence. Antony was fluent in his story now, so there was really no need for questions, but even after he had finished speaking it was some seconds before the detective brought himself to comment. 'You've got it all off pat, haven't you?' he said then, admiringly.

'Is that all you've got to say about it?' Antony was nettled. 'I'm deadly serious about this,' he added. 'There's Philip Brady to think about, or had you forgotten?'

'I hadn't forgotten. What do you think I'm here for, Mr. Maitland?'

Antony chose to take the question literally. 'To look into Harley's goings on, including the possibility of his having killed Dobell himself and framed Brady.'

'That's precisely it. And I shall do it to the best of my ability, you needn't worry about that. So what I think at this juncture doesn't really matter. May I ask what your own intentions are?'

'To leave Brady's fate in your hands, at least for the present.'

'That's sensible of you.' Sykes nodded approvingly. 'You're going back to town then?'

'I am. But I've been very frank with you, Chief Inspector. Don't you think you owe me a little frankness in return?'

Sykes took that cautiously. 'In what way?'

'You've been here since last night – '

'Too late to do anything except talk to the Chief Constable.'

'Well, anyway, you've been in action all the morning. Don't tell me you haven't formed some ideas.'

'I appreciate the problem sufficiently to know that it requires careful handling, very careful.' Antony made an impatient gesture and got up from his perch on the stool in front of the dressing-table. 'But I will tell you one thing,'

Sykes added placidly. 'The witnesses I've seen stick to their stories. All but this Miss Pershing you're reported to be interested in. She seems to have disappeared.'

That brought Antony, who had begun to pace his favourite track from the bathroom door to the foot of the bed, to an immediate halt. 'How do you know?' he demanded.

'It was ten o'clock when I got to the block of flats where she lives. The janitor – superintendent he calls himself – saw her leaving with a suitcase just after nine. She took her car; so far neither it nor she has been traced.'

'But . . . doesn't that make you think? She heard of Harley's murder –'

'Of Harley's death,' Sykes corrected him.

'Murder . . . death . . . whatever you like! Doesn't that make you think?' he asked again.

'It doesn't make me jump to conclusions,' Sykes told him repressively. 'She was upset at having to give evidence against the man she loves, and felt she must have a change of scene. Doesn't that fit just as well as your version?'

'If you knew the lady –'

'What then?'

'She isn't in love with Brady.'

'So you tell me, Mr. Maitland. I should like the opportunity of judging for myself.' Sykes got up as he spoke.

'But you can't leave it like that! Hasn't anything been done about Superintendent Harley's affairs?'

'Enquiries are being made. Well, I talked to his widow,' said Sykes, relenting.

'A difficult task, I can see that.'

'Not perhaps so difficult as you think. She was perfectly discreet in what she actually said, but I gained the distinct impression that she wasn't altogether heart-broken by what had happened.'

'Peter Gibson told me she had money. That's what Northdean thinks.'

'There was certainly money somewhere.'

'Well, do you think she knew what Harley was up to?'

'You're going too fast for me, Mr. Maitland. We don't know that he was up to anything.'

'If you ask m-me –' It wasn't often that Antony found himself moved to a loss of temper by the detective's natural caution, but he was more worried even than he had admitted, and he was close to it now. Perhaps it was as well that at that moment the telephone shrilled. He broke off with an angry exclamation and strode across the room to pick up the receiver. A moment later he turned and held it out to his companion. 'It's for you,' he said.

'I took the liberty of telling them at the station where I should be,' said Sykes as he came across the room, not hurrying himself, but not wasting any time either. Antony went to the window, rammed his hands into his pockets, and stood looking out.

There followed a somewhat lengthy conversation, to which Sykes's contribution was mainly monosyllabic. At last he replaced the receiver in his usual methodical way and turned back to the room again.

'You might find this interesting, Mr. Maitland,' he said. 'Sir Richard declines to commit himself positively: I don't think he could be persuaded to swear to it in court, but he is of the opinion that Harley was dead before his car went over the edge of the quarry.'

'How did he die then?' Antony had forgotten his annoyance and his tone was eager.

'Most likely of a broken neck. That, Sir Richard thinks, was the first of the injuries. There were others, of course, when the car went over, but he believes that they were made after death.'

'Now we're getting somewhere! If this doesn't change your mind, Chief Inspector –'

'It certainly seems to be to some degree a confirmation of your theory,' Sykes admitted. But Antony for the moment was too jubilant to be irritated all over again by the careful wording of this statement.

'It means you'll really put your heart into the enquiry,' he asserted. '*Now* will you answer my question? Does Mrs. Harley know what was going on?'

Sykes looked at him for a long moment, but even now he wasn't willing to concede the point altogether. 'Assuming for the sake of argument that your theory is correct,' he began, and then suddenly threw in his hand. 'She knew,' he said positively.

Antony wasn't going to be so incautious as to display his gratification at obtaining this admission. 'If she knew Mr. X – ' he started soberly, and then broke off, because the conclusion of that sentence must be as obvious to his companion as it was to him.

'That's another matter. But I doubt if any man in the situation you describe would be quite so confiding.'

'Yes, I doubt it too. Ah well, who lives may learn. We shall just have to wait and see.'

'There's one thing that's puzzling me, Mr. Maitland – '

'Only one?' asked Antony flippantly.

' – if Mr. X was so careful about preserving his anonymity, except from Harley, for instance, and other men of similar rank in his organisation, who – when it came to cutting his losses as you call it – did he trust to bring about Harley's demise?'

'I've thought about that, of course. He didn't do it himself, that's certain.'

'Not the type?'

'That, of course, but neither would he have had the physical strength. Harley was a powerful man.'

'He must obviously have been taken by surprise. If somebody was in the car with him, somebody who was in a position to give him orders, who then ordered him to pull in to the side of the road . . . it isn't too difficult, if you know just how to set about it.'

'No,' said Maitland. For the moment Sykes had the impression that his mind was far away. 'Not Mr. X,' he said then, bringing himself back to the present with what seemed to be an effort. 'But he had at least one associate who knew, if he knew nothing else, that his employer was up to no good. The man who escorted me to his doorstep at gun point, whom he referred to, as far as I remember, as Kenneth.'

'You think this man – ?'

'If he is still employed by Mr. X, I should imagine he is a good deal more sure of himself today than he was six years ago. Older in sin, you might say. But I'm not wedded to the idea. If Mr. X has one associate, not necessarily in his complete confidence but available for any dirty work that needs doing, there may be others.'

'Yes, that sounds very likely,' said Sykes, committing himself to an opinion a little more definitely than was his custom. He was still standing with his back to the bedside table where the telephone rested, but now he stooped to pick up the briefcase he had laid down on the bed and said in a sombre tone, 'Do you think this is an easy problem you've laid in my lap, Mr. Maitland?'

'On the contrary, I'm just beginning to realise how hopeless it is,' said Antony, only too well aware that to convince Sykes of the rightness of his theories, as he seemed to have done, went nowhere near to proving them. 'If there was any connecting link at all . . . but there isn't.'

'Well, I must thank you for giving me so much of your time,' said Sykes, a stickler, as ever, for the proprieties. 'I'll be getting along now.'

'You'll let me know if there's anything . . . if anything turns up?'

'Of course I will.' That was said with more warmth than the detective usually allowed himself. 'Or if you have any more bright ideas, Mr. Maitland, you know where to find me.'

On that note they parted. The afternoon train had long

gone on its way so Antony, with more time to kill, strolled round to Peter Gibson's office – could he help it if it was tea-time again? – and gave him a detailed account of all that had transpired. 'You might let Brady know we're not deserting him,' he said in parting. 'If you can do so without raising any false hopes.'

'I'll try,' said Peter heavily. Obviously the prospect did not enchant him, so that Antony said defensively,

'If there was anything to be done here at the moment, I'd stay. But there's nothing I can do that Sykes can't do a hundred times better. Besides – '

'You have this idea,' said Gibson, and now he sounded more hopeful, so that suddenly Maitland's mood exploded again into anger.

'D-don't c-count on it,' he said, as forcefully as he could. 'I s-see now I shouldn't have s-said anything. It looks p-pretty hopeless to me.'

Perhaps it was as well that Peter Gibson, left staring at the closing door, had sufficient perception to realise that the anger, though momentarily bitter, was almost entirely self-directed.

II

Jenny was delayed in the kitchen, waiting for the coffee to drip. Sir Nicholas, in his favourite armchair, suspended his leisurely preparations for the enjoyment of a cigar, glanced suspiciously at the door, and remarked, 'The child is worried. Without reason, as I believe . . . for the moment.'

Vera, too, gave an anxious look at the doorway. 'Don't like the sound of that,' she said gruffly.

'I mean, as I explained to you . . . well, I don't know what he has in mind, what his reason really is for coming home,' said Sir Nicholas, with rather less than his usual clarity.

Miss Langhorne considered. 'Ought to trust him,' she said at length.

Sir Nicholas smiled at her, a trifle wryly. 'In a way, that's the whole trouble,' he told her. 'I can trust him to do what he thinks is right, but sometimes I admit I wish . . . he has this built-in sensitivity where people are concerned. I remind him of the occasions he has been wrong – for the good of his soul, you can understand that, I am sure – but far more often even the wildest of his guesses have turned out to be correct.'

'You think he has some idea as to how Mr. X may be traced?'

'He said as much, quite early in the proceedings, and then I think he regretted it because he hasn't mentioned it again.'

'May tell you when he gets home.'

'I doubt it,' Sir Nicholas grumbled, but Jenny came in just then with the coffee pot and his complaint was shelved for the moment.

Much later in the evening, when the record player had just finished Haydn's Divertimento for Cello and Orchestra, he asked idly, 'Have you never thought of moving to London, Miss Langhorne? The opportunities for concert-going . . . and I suppose, like the rest of us, you prefer your music live rather than recorded, however excellent the recording may be.'

'Thought about it, of course, never could afford it,' said Vera matter-of-factly.

'Well, I realise your practice has always been on the West Midland Circuit, but I can't help feeling you would find life here more – more fulfilling,' said Sir Nicholas.

Vera gave him one of her grim smiles, but obviously felt she had said all there was to be said on the subject. Jenny, uncurling herself from her place on the sofa, said impulsively, 'It would be nice if you weren't so far away.' She went across the room to fetch the brandy bottle; they were drinking Sir Nicholas's special cognac that evening, in honour of the visitor, who now seemed a little embarrassed as she always did when anything in the nature of a compliment was paid.

'Good train service,' she said. And then, thinking perhaps

that that had sounded a bit abrupt, 'Know I always like to come here, Jenny.'

And the truth of that is, thought Jenny, you can't afford the train fare very often. She wondered for a moment whether to put another record on, but Uncle Nick seemed in a talkative mood so she came back to her seat again.

'Have you always lived in Chedcombe?' he was asking.

'All my life.' Perhaps his mood had infected Vera a little, in any event she went on without any prompting. 'Nice little place. Bit narrow-minded, but it was a long time before I realised that.'

'When your house was burned down,' said Sir Nicholas, obviously troubled by the recollection.

'Gutted,' Vera corrected him. 'Not altogether a bad thing, either. Got some new stereo equipment out of it . . . house was over-furnished anyway. And I'd always wanted a *chaise-longue*.' She looked from one to the other of her companions, inviting their amusement. 'Got that too.'

'Still – ' began Sir Nicholas. But Jenny was following her own train of thought.

'It was a horrible thing to do,' she said indignantly.

'Natural,' said Vera, who obviously felt less animosity about the affair than her audience did. 'Whole town was against Fran Gifford, you know. Didn't like me for defending her, and particularly for bringing in a stranger.'

'I remember that,' said Jenny, sighing. Sir Nicholas gave her a quick look, but when he spoke again it was to Miss Langhorne.

'You're very tolerant,' he said. 'Far more tolerant than I should be in similar circumstances. I wonder though . . . what made you choose the law?'

'What made you choose it, Sir Nicholas?'

'I never considered any other career. Both my father and grandfather – '

'Same with me.' Vera waited a moment before replying, until she was sure he had nothing to add. 'Father, I mean.

149

He was a solicitor, not a barrister, but he had ambitions on my behalf. Often thought though, a solicitor's office might have suited me better.'

'Now there, my dear Vera, I cannot agree with you. You have chosen to remain at the junior Bar – '

'Couldn't afford the change,' said Miss Langhorne, incurably honest.

' – but your grasp of each case is excellent, as I have had several opportunities of observing, and your courtroom manner – '

'Blunt,' said Vera, and smiled again.

'Well, perhaps,' said Sir Nicholas, rather feebly, Jenny thought. But if Vera was offended by his agreement she gave no sign.

'Father never lived to brief me,' she said. 'Pity, that. He and Mother both died in a car crash when I was twenty. Enough money, though, to finish my training and put my young brother through school.'

'There were just the two of you?'

'Yes. No sisters, or cousins, or aunts either,' amplified Vera with a flash of humour.

'You never told us you had a brother,' said Jenny.

'He was killed in the war, right at the beginning.' Her tone was as gruff as ever.

'I'm sorry,' said Jenny and Sir Nicholas simultaneously. But Vera wasn't waiting for sympathy.

'Long time ago,' she said. 'Still miss him. He was in the retreat, you know, and killed at Dunkirk just as he was embarking. A lot of men went the same way.'

'I have never found that a grief shared is any less a grief,' said Sir Nicholas thoughtfully. 'Had you already been called to the Bar at that time?'

'I'm sixty-one,' said Vera cheerfully. 'Work it out for yourself,' she invited.

'I shall endeavour to do so.' Sir Nicholas put down the stub of his second cigar of the evening with regret and then drank the last of his brandy. 'I shall leave you now,' he said then. 'Are you going to sit up for Antony, Jenny?'

'I thought I would.'

'As it is already half-past eleven you will not have long to wait. Good night, Miss Langhorne. I shall look forward to a further instalment of your memoirs.'

'Talk too much,' said Vera sadly, after he had gone. Jenny, who was piling cups and glasses onto a tray, stopped her task for a moment and laughed. 'Nothing of the kind,' she asserted. 'If anything, you know, it's just the opposite.'

'Sir Nicholas said –'

'He meant *exactly* what he said,' said Jenny firmly, and was pretty sure as she spoke that it was the simple truth. 'Don't you understand, your friends like to hear all about you, about your family, and about the things you're interested in.'

'Not very entertaining,' said Vera, and obviously believed the truth of what she was saying. She went up to bed soon after that, in the attic that the Maitlands had made into quite a comfortable room, but though Jenny had argued with her in the meantime Jenny wasn't at all sure that her efforts had met with much success. She was thoughtful, for more reasons than one, as she settled herself to wait for her husband.

SATURDAY, 29th MAY

I

In the event, it was nearly one o'clock when Antony came in, and Jenny saw at once that he was far too tired for conversation. She waited until the next morning at breakfast, therefore, to tell him that Roger and Meg were coming that afternoon. 'And Uncle Nick is taking Vera to tea at Claridges,' she added. Antony took another piece of toast. He was still looking desperately weary.

'His idea of being tactful, I suppose,' he said. Vera was not yet down.

'Oh, do you think so?' asked Jenny. For some reason she sounded amused, and Antony looked at her curiously.

'What else? I'd rather talk to Roger alone, as a matter of fact.'

'That's not really kind, Antony.'

'What do you mean?'

'Uncle Nick told me everything,' said Jenny, making it sound dramatic. 'Including the fact that you had an idea you thought might lead you to Mr. X.'

'It isn't really quite so definite as that, love,' Antony protested. 'Anyway, I don't mind you and Meg being there when I talk to Roger.'

'I should hope not. But Uncle Nick will probably die of frustrated curiosity, let alone how Vera will feel.'

Maitland grinned. 'She, at least, wouldn't badger me about it,' he asserted. 'I'll tell you what . . . if Roger thinks there's anything in this idea of mine I'll put them in the picture at dinner time. That is – '

'Uncle Nick's coming to dinner, of course,' said Jenny.

'The thing is, you see, love, half the time I think I'll be making a fool of myself by propounding this idea at all, and I'm not awfully keen on having Uncle Nick laugh it out of court. I'll try it on Roger first.'

'That's a good idea,' Jenny agreed. She looked as if she had something else on her mind, but just then they heard Vera's step on the stairs and the moment for confidences was lost.

II

Roger and Meg Farrell (she was better known to the theatre-going public as Margaret Hamilton) were perhaps the Maitlands' closest friends. Meg was small and slightly built and still wore her dark hair twisted round her head in a long plait. In fact, she had really changed very little with the years, except that she had acquired an elegance she had not had when first she came to London; and that the years had taught her to hide an exceedingly forthright nature under a layer of affectation. Roger was a sturdily built man, very near Antony in age, with blue eyes, straight, sandy hair, and a forceful manner. There was, it must be admitted, a piratical air about him, which ill-became a member of the Stock Exchange; but he had also, as his friends well knew, an odd streak of sensitivity about him which made him extremely responsive to other people's moods.

They arrived in good time that afternoon, which was probably Roger's doing, but he showed no signs of undue curiosity. Meg, however, hardly gave them time to get seated again before she was asking, 'You said you'd never go to Westhampton again, Antony. What took you there this time?'

'It's a long story. Would you mind dreadfully, Meg, if I reserved it for a later date?'

'I'd mind, of course, darling. You know I'm simply

seething with curiosity.' She stopped there and looked at him, and then went on, dropping her teasing tone. 'No, of course it doesn't matter. Just tell us what you want of Roger.'

Without embarking on the whole story, which he was tired of telling, it was hard to know where to begin. 'I have to remind you at least of what I once told you about my meeting with a man whom even Uncle Nick has agreed to call Mr. X.'

'But that was years ago,' said Meg, and

'The uncrowned king of the diamond smugglers,' said Roger thoughtfully.

'You do remember,' said Antony with relief. 'Well, he's cropped up again in the background to this matter . . . at least, I'm pretty sure he has and Uncle Nick agrees with me. But the devil of it is he's murdered the man – or I should say, had him killed – who was the only link between him and Northdean.'

'I should have thought,' said Meg, a little primly, 'that that was all to the good.'

'My client – or rather, Uncle Nick's client now – is in prison, and I want to get him out.'

'Would finding Mr. X achieve that, do you think?'

'I don't know. But he ought to be stopped, Roger, he's behaving with utter ruthlessness. When you hear the whole story you'll understand.'

'But I don't see,' said Meg, 'how Roger can help you. And if you really think he can help you find this man,' she added, glancing at Jenny, 'I'm not at all sure that I want him to.'

Antony was beginning to looked harassed. 'I'll tell you what I shall tell Uncle Nick, what I've already told Jenny. I don't intend to take any action myself, even if we do succeed in identifying him. I've met the man once, and that was quite enough. I shall just tell Sykes, and leave it up to him.'

'That's all very fine,' Meg began. And then she stopped and looked at Jenny again. 'I don't want to be tiresome,' she said uncertainly, 'if you really mean what you say.'

'I really mean it,' he assured her. But he hadn't relaxed yet and his voice was still strained as he went on. 'Have I your permission, *darling*, to put my point to your husband?'

Meg, who knew perfectly well that he only addressed her in that manner when his patience was near to breaking point, assumed a martyred expression and said simply, 'Yes,' in a small voice. At which Antony, whose ill-temper never lasted for long, especially with someone he was so fond of, grinned and said,

'Right!' in a business-like tone.

Jenny said, 'The kettle must be boiling, I'll make the tea,' and went away to do so.

Looking after her, Meg said contritely, 'I didn't mean to rock the boat, darling, but you do realise she's worried sick by all this, don't you?'

Antony, having been on the verge of losing his temper once, wasn't going to do so again. He did, however, give a rather despairing look in Roger's direction. 'Of course he realises it, Meg,' said Roger briskly. 'But you know Jenny, she'd never try to stop him from doing what he thinks he has to do.'

'That doesn't mean you have to take advantage of her forbearance.' Meg's tone was uncharacteristically waspish, and she herself seemed just as startled by the fact as either of the others. 'I didn't mean that . . . really,' she said at once. 'I know what Roger said: what you think you *have* to do.'

As an *amende* it was honourable enough, but it led to a short silence. This was broken by Roger, who got up and made for the door. 'I'll go and carry the tray,' he said over his shoulder as he went.

Maitland, having won his point, he thought, had for the moment nothing further to say. Meg was silent too, but luckily they knew each other far too well for this to be an embarrassment.

When the others returned and the tea was poured and Jenny's scones had circulated, Antony said without further

155

preliminaries, 'I have one clue to Mr. X's identity. Something he said of himself. I don't know the street he lives in, only that his house is number ten. I made a sort of feeble joke about that, wondering if I should find myself at a cabinet meeting, and in reply he said quite seriously that "though the gentleman in Downing Street is better known than I am, he is a good deal less influential". At the time it didn't mean anything to me, and as you've probably guessed I wasn't too anxious to make his further acquaintance. But the last few days I've been giving the matter a good deal of thought, and this is what I've come up with. He used the word influence, but he was talking about power. What does that mean to you?'

Meg said, 'I pass.' Roger frowned over the question for a moment and then ventured, 'It seems he was deliberately excluding political power.'

'Yes, I think so too. It occurred to me that for real power in the world today you have to look for money.' He paused, and then said, in an oddly tentative way, 'Is that being very cynical?'

Roger said slowly, thinking it out, 'You know, you may be right about that.'

'It's a forlorn hope at best.' Antony seemed determined on self-denigration.

'But where do I come in?'

'I thought you might know . . . might be able to suggest . . . someone to whom the description might apply.'

'That's rather a tall order, isn't it?'

'Do you think I don't realise that? But think it over,' Antony urged.

'Well, I suppose . . . one of the merchant bankers. One of the houses with one man at the top, not a Board of Directors. I'm just thinking aloud,' said Roger, suddenly and uncharacteristically diffident in his turn. 'But, look here,' – he was warming to the task that had been set him now – 'why don't

I ask old Tremlett. Or do you think – he's a powerful man himself – that he might be your Mr. X?'

Antony smiled at him. 'That's one thing I'm sure of . . . that he isn't, I mean. I've seen his picture often enough in the papers. That's another thing I know about Mr. X, though it's only helpful in a negative way. He never allows himself to be photographed.'

'What do you think of my idea?'

'Would Mr. Tremlett be helpful?'

'Oh, yes, I think so. He knew my father. Not that that's much of a recommendation,' Roger added, but without the bitterness that would once have coloured his voice, 'but he thinks it is, and who am I to disillusion him?'

'Well then . . . make it a hypothetical case, Roger. If you can manage without putting him completely in the picture – '

'I don't know the full story myself,' Roger reminded him.

'That's right, you don't.' He glanced at Jenny, who rarely interrupted, and then at Meg, who did, but who now seemed strangely subdued. 'I suppose I'd better tell you after all,' he said resignedly. 'It started, I suppose, when Sykes asked me to represent Philip Brady in a suit for wrongful arrest that was being brought against him . . .'

III

Vera Langhorne and Sir Nicholas returned from their expedition in excellent spirits, rather later than the Maitlands had expected them. Dinner was already in the oven, Meg had left for the theatre, and Roger had gone, by arrangement, to see his old friend, Mr. Tremlett. Jenny brought out the glasses and Antony produced a bottle of Tio Pepe; it hadn't escaped his notice that Vera, under his uncle's tutelage, was developing a very gentlemanly taste in wine. Having put his problem squarely onto someone else's shoulders he ought to have been feeling some relief, but in spite of a day spent mostly in idleness there had been far too much talk, and he was feeling tired and depressed.

Vera, however, was in an unusually talkative mood, her worries of the previous night apparently forgotten. 'Seen more of London today than I ever have before,' she informed them. 'The Bank of England, and the Tower, and the Abbey, and Parliament –'

'Where, I regret to say, we observed several couples disporting themselves in a manner highly unsuited to the dignity of the profession,' Sir Nicholas put in austerely.

'Necking,' said Vera, whose vocabulary in some ways had never been brought up to date.

She exchanged a smile with Sir Nicholas, who murmured, 'Precisely,' and sipped his sherry in an appreciative way. Antony, who knew only too well his uncle's dislike of the vernacular, ventured on a comment.

'Not exactly on your way home,' he said.

'We came home,' admitted Sir Nicholas blandly, 'by a circuitous route.'

'It would seem so.' Antony's tone was dry, but it seemed that the older man was in an impregnably amiable mood.

'The driver of the taxicab was obliging enough to take us slowly round all these points of interest,' he said.

'Also saw the Abbey, and the Houses of Parliament, and the Horse Guards, and Buckingham Palace,' Vera put in enthusiastically. 'And the Albert Hall and the Royal Festival Hall . . . education in itself.'

'Yes, I suppose so.' Maitland sounded as if he found the catalogue a little stunning. He glanced at Jenny and found her smiling quietly to herself.

'But what we really want to know' – Vera glanced at Sir Nicholas as though inviting his support – 'is, has your friend Roger Farrell been here, and what did he have to say?'

If his uncle had put the question he might have returned a short answer. As it was, 'He's been here all right,' Antony said, 'and he's gone away to wrestle with the problem. I may hear from him later tonight.'

'But – ' said Vera, and stopped as though she couldn't think what else to say. Sir Nicholas roused himself to take over the inquisition. 'I really think you must tell us, my dear boy,' he said, in the tone that meant he wasn't going to be satisfied with anything less than a full reply, 'exactly what this idea of yours is.'

'I've done enough talking for one day,' said Antony, unresponsive.

'I'll tell them if you like,' Jenny said innocently. Her explanations were notoriously complicated and Antony, taking the offer at its real value, laughed for the first time that day.

'Yes, I know you think I should tell them, love. I'll do it if I must.' And, of course, after propounding his thoughts so recently to Roger, it didn't take long to express them again.

There was a silence when he had finished. Miss Langhorne was looking troubled. At length Sir Nicholas said consideringly, 'I think there may be some merit in this idea of yours, Antony.' Maitland was far too surprised by this endorsement of his opinion to make any immediate reply, and after a moment his uncle went on. 'What do you think about it, Miss Langhorne?'

'I think – ' said Vera, and hesitated. 'There's one point you mentioned about your talk with Mr. X when you told me about it at the time, Antony. Didn't comment on it . . . thought it as well to forget the whole business.'

'Something I've forgotten?' said Antony. For the moment at least his weariness seemed to have left him, and he sounded eager.

'Something you didn't mention having told Mr. Farrell,' said Vera, anxious to be exact. 'Said Mr. X used the phrase "not proven". Struck me at the time he might be a Scotsman.'

'Good lord! Yes, I remember that now. If Roger comes up with some names – '

'You say he has gone to consult Joseph Tremlett. That's flying high indeed.'

'Well, he knows him, you see.'

'So I suppose. You should be grateful to Miss Langhorne for her suggestion, Antony. It may prove extremely helpful ... to the police.'

His meaning was not lost upon his nephew. 'You're quite right, Uncle Nick, if we succeed in identifying Mr. X I shall unload the whole thing on them.'

'Hope you mean that,' said Vera. 'Should regret my intervention if you don't.' It was obvious to Jenny, valiantly concealing her own anxiety, that Vera Langhorne already knew her husband well enough not to trust him an inch.

IV

They had barely finished dinner when the visitor arrived. Antony was searching for his recording of *Messiah*, which for some reason he always associated with Vera's visits, and Jenny was pouring coffee, when Gibbs, Sir Nicholas's butler, came labouring upstairs to inform them that there was a young lady to see Mr. Maitland. He managed to make this sound faintly scandalous. 'Well, who is she?' said Antony, succeeding well enough in hiding his impatience. It was never any good pointing out to Gibbs that he could just as well have used the house phone.

'A Miss Pershing, Mr. Maitland.'

That brought him up with a jerk. He relinquished his search and came back to stand on the hearthrug in front of the now empty grate. 'What do we do about that, Uncle Nick?'

'In the circumstances, I think you must see her,' said Sir Nicholas without any hesitation at all.

'Even though she's a prosecution witness?'

'I think the fact that her life may be in danger, if she has any inkling of Mr. X's identity, must override the conventions in this instance.'

'Y-yes. I suppose I'd better see her alone,' he added, but his uncle did not, as he had hoped, contradict him.

'It is you she is asking for, after all,' said Sir Nicholas unsympathetically.

'All right. Thank you, Gibbs, I'll go straight down.' He made for the door and the old butler followed him more slowly.

He found Moira Pershing pacing the floor between desk and window in his uncle's study. Unexpectedly, she came across the room to him with her hands held out, as though she was greeting an old friend. She was as elegantly turned out as ever, but there was no laughter in her eyes today; he thought she had been crying. Still unexpectedly she said, in that husky voice of hers, 'Mr. Maitland! It's good of you to see me.'

Because there seemed nothing else to be done he took her hands and led her to one of the deep leather chairs, the one that Sir Nicholas favoured. 'Sit down, Miss Pershing, and tell me what I can do for you.'

'I don't think anybody can help me really.' She released his hands with apparently some reluctance and sat down obediently in the big chair. He thought perhaps she needed the reassurance of some human contact and remained standing looking down at her, not so far away as the other side of the hearth. He was quite sure now that she had been crying; not only that, but the tears were still not very far away.

'You know, of course,' he said, 'that I'm contravening the conventions by talking to you. A prosecution witness – '

'But that's what I wanted to tell you. I'm not that any more. I want to confirm Philip's alibi.'

'I . . . see.' It wasn't in the least true, but the words served to conceal his bewilderment.

'Don't you understand? He was with me, as he said, until well past midnight.'

'I understand, but I think I should point out to you, Miss Pershing, that the prosecution won't be very happy with this change in your evidence. You'll be subject to cross-examination, which is likely to be severe.'

'You mean, they'll throw in my face what I said in my previous statement. I can't help that. You're taking this very calmly, Mr. Maitland.' She obviously felt some sense of injury about this. 'I thought you'd be pleased.'

'At the prospect of clearing Philip Brady . . . I am pleased, of course.' He had been leaning one shoulder against the mantel, but now he straightened himself and his eyes became more intent. 'There's one slight reservation in my mind, however. Can I trust you?'

The question seemed to startle her. 'Why on earth should I be here at all if I weren't telling the truth?' she demanded.

'I don't know,' he admitted. 'But you've lied once, who's to say you won't change your mind about your testimony a second time?'

'I won't, Mr. Maitland, really I won't.' His tone had been quite dispassionate, but his words had gone home.

'You will forgive me, Miss Pershing. I should like some further assurance on that score.'

'What do you want me to say?'

'Why you lied in the first place, and why you have come to me now.'

'I was going to tell you anyway.'

'That's good. Take your time, but tell me everything.'

'Shall I have to repeat all this in court?'

'That would be up to the judge. My uncle would do his best to protect you from the opposing counsel, of course.' His tone was formal, but then suddenly he relented. 'Don't worry, Miss Pershing, if you'll repeat your statement to the police the matter may never come to trial.'

'But there's been one hearing.'

'That may make things a little difficult for you – '

'That's what I thought.'

'– but you've come forward voluntarily, and if you can help us to get to the truth of the matter that would be taken into consideration.'

'Not a very bright prospect.' She shrugged, as though dismissing the thought. 'Well, it doesn't matter really. Nothing matters since Charlie died. Except, perhaps, getting even with *him*.'

Too many lines there to pursue them all at once. 'Charlie?' he queried gently. She scrabbled in her handbag for a moment, produced a handkerchief and blew her nose prosaically, but when she looked up at him again her eyes were still swimming with tears.

'Superintendent Charles Harley,' she explained. 'I suppose I must tell you, you won't understand unless I do, I'd been his mistress for the past four years. Only it was more than that. It was a permanent and very – very strong relationship.'

'I see,' said Maitland again. This time, at least, he meant it. 'I do understand this is painful for you, but I need to know everything you can tell me.'

'I realise that.' He tried for a moment to think back to the bright, self-confident young woman he had met in Philip Brady's apartment, and found it almost impossible. 'I realise too,' she went on, and he saw that each word was an effort, 'that I shall have to go to the police, but I thought if I talked to you first you might be willing to help me about that.'

'Anything I can do,' he said, and tried the effect of a lighter tone. 'So long as your story as a whole is convincing enough; I don't want Sykes thinking I've been doing a spot of subornation of perjury myself.'

She greeted the suggestion with a rather watery smile, but said questioningly, 'Sykes?'

'Chief Inspector Sykes of Scotland Yard.'

'The paper said they'd been called in.'

'But you didn't wait to see him.'

'No. Don't you see, I didn't know what to do when I heard Charlie was dead. That's why I thought I'd get away for a while, until I could think things out. And then I was . . . I am . . . rather frightened. I suppose that, more than anything else, is why I'm here.'

'You're quite safe in this house,' he said, and hoped it was the truth. 'But I'm waiting, you know, for you to tell me – '

'Yes, of course.' She used the handkerchief again, this time to dab her eyes. 'I was at a loose end when I met Charlie, and we got on together right away.'

'Where did you meet?'

'At the theatre, of all places, in the bar during the interval. I was with a girl friend . . . that doesn't matter.'

'And who was the Superintendent with?'

'He was on his own. We just . . . well, sometimes you know right away if someone is right for you. He came up to London quite often by himself; he didn't get on with his wife.'

'I have been wondering, since you told me about your association with him, why they stayed together.'

'I wondered about that myself, at first. It was only later that I realised she knew too much about him for him ever to be able to leave her. As for her . . . there was plenty of money, you see, and I dare say she liked that. I know I did,' she added with a sort of half-hearted attempt at defiance. 'That was one of the first things that became obvious, you see, when we got to know each other. I moved into a new flat, much more elegant than the one I'd had, and . . . oh, I admit, I revelled in the situation. But after a while, of course, I began to realise that he wasn't footing the bill out of his pay as a policeman.'

'So you asked him?'

'Wouldn't you have done? We were pretty close by then, of course – I told you that – and funnily enough he didn't seem to mind the question. In fact, I think it was a relief to him to have someone to confide in. He said his wife knew what he was doing, but I expect it was a long time since he'd talked to her about anything that mattered.'

'Now you do interest me, Miss Pershing. Try to remember everything he told you.'

'Well, he said there was a way of making money that didn't harm anybody else. He said it didn't involve him in actually taking any action, only organising other people.'

'Did he tell you what this way of making money was?'

'Only after I asked him rather persistently. He said there was a lot of diamond smuggling going on, some to Iron Curtain countries who were stock-piling them; I never understood that properly, what they wanted them for. But there was also a good business to be done on behalf of people wanting to take currency out of the country, this way it could be done inconspicuously. And you know, Mr. Maitland, there didn't seem much harm in it. I mean, why shouldn't people do what they like with their own?'

There was a good deal he could have said about that, but he judged it best to be silent. Instead he asked, as casually as he could, 'What happened when Dobell and Irving were arrested? They were guilty, weren't they?'

'Oh yes, he told me all about that. They were his men, he said, and he had to look after them. As a matter of fact, he was absolutely furious with Philip for interfering, and particularly when he said he wasn't going to drop the matter after their acquittal.'

'That acquittal was stage-managed by Superintendent Harley?'

'It was. He was rather pleased with the arrangements he made, liked talking about them. But, of course, he knew he ould trust me.'

And was very much in love with you, Antony thought. So much seemed to be obvious. He also thought it obvious that the girl was completely amoral, while having at the same time an odd streak of conventionality. Aloud he said, 'Was it his decision to start the wrongful arrest proceedings?'

'No, but he thought it was a splendid idea. He thought it would discourage Philip as nothing else could. That was when – '

'Just a minute. Something I've been wanting to get clear. He wasn't the head of the organisation then?'

'He was in charge of the Northdean area, but he said there were – branches, he called them – all over the country, and on the continent as well. One man headed the organisation, and only one man in each branch knew him.'

'Superintendent Harley knew who his principal was?'

'Yes.'

'Did he ever tell you – ?'

'Nothing . . . Nothing! He said it would be too dangerous.'

That was all very well as far as it went, provided Mr. X was confident of his subordinate's discretion. 'You were going to tell me, I think, how you came to be in Northdean yourself.'

'Charlie asked me to go there, to get a flat and get to know Philip somehow. That wasn't really difficult, you know.'

'I imagine not. But why, Miss Pershing? I don't understand why, at that time, he should want to involve you with Inspector Brady.'

'He said further action might be called for. I think that was the other man's idea too, but Charlie was always one to be careful. He couldn't have survived in Northdean if he wasn't; for that matter, he couldn't have kept his association with me secret, as I'm sure it was.'

'Do you think that at that time the murder of Dobell was contemplated?'

'I think, but I'm not sure, that was because you were brought into the case. Killing two birds with one stone, Charlie called it, fixing Philip and making sure you lost interest in him as a client.'

'But that part of the plan didn't work.'

'Charlie was furious about that, too. He said he was going to consult the other man and see what could be done about you.' She stopped there, and then added in a desolate tone, 'Only he was killed first.'

It was insane to feel a compulsion to apologise for not being the one to be murdered. Antony said slowly, 'And so you came to me.'

'That's right.'

'Why?'

'Because – don't you see? – nothing I tell you can hurt Charlie now. And I want that man to be caught and punished. He killed him, I'm sure of it.'

'Or had him killed. Yes, I think so too. There's the added bonus too that your giving him an alibi will get Philip off a murder charge.'

'I suppose it will.' It was obvious that this aspect of the matter was of very little concern to her. Predictably she added, 'I don't really care about that, one way or the other,' and Antony noted with a shiver down his spine that the statement seemed quite sincere.

'Well, I care,' he couldn't refrain from saying, and spoke more abruptly than he intended, so that Moira looked at him enquiringly, as though she were wondering what made him tick. To bring back her attention to the matter in hand he said urgently, 'Isn't there anything else you can tell me about the one you call "the other man"?'

'I've thought and thought, and if there was anything I'd tell you. He lives in London, but that isn't very much help, is it? And he . . . Charlie respected him, I could tell that. Said he'd never put a foot wrong so long as he followed instructions.'

That was a disappointment, though no more than he had expected; but you had to count your gains, and Philip Brady's freedom was what he had been working for, after all. He said, speaking slowly again, thinking it out, 'What are we going to do with you now, Miss Pershing?'

'I'll go back to my flat. I kept it on when I came to Northdean. That was only a temporary arrangement, and money never seemed to be an object with Charlie, you know.'

'I don't really think that's a good idea. Harley didn't tell you about "the other man", but he may have told him about you.'

'You mean . . . I'm in danger?'

'You could be. It's not worth taking a chance on it.'

She had rather a wry smile for that. 'Is it my safety you're concerned with, or Philip's acquittal?'

He stopped again to consider. 'Both, I hope,' he said at last, smiling. 'Will you wait here, Miss Pershing, while I talk to my uncle?'

'Someone told me that the lawyer in the Magistrate's Court was your uncle.'

'Sir Nicholas Harding. This is his study we're using. He's upstairs in my quarters this evening.'

'He doesn't like me.'

'You're on the same side now . . . remember? In case you're nervous' – she looked it – 'he wouldn't cross-examine his own witness.'

'I suppose not. All right, Mr. Maitland, I'll wait for you, but I don't know whether you're being sensible, or making a great deal of fuss about nothing.'

He rather wondered that himself, but the first thing Sir Nicholas said when he had finished a brief relation of what had transpired was, 'You haven't let her go home?'

'No. I thought – '

'On no account must she leave this house until Chief Inspector Sykes has seen her. You'd better telephone him, Antony, and tell him to come back to town first thing in the morning.'

'And meanwhile?'

'We will put her in my spare bedroom. Mrs. Stokes and Jenny between them can find her what she needs for tonight. Will you see to it, my dear?' Jenny got up obediently.

'I'll take her something to read,' she said. 'Do you think she'll argue about staying, Antony?'

'I shouldn't think so, love. I didn't actually suggest it, but she seemed quite resigned to doing whatever we thought was wise.'

'All right then.' Jenny went across to the bookshelves. 'I wish all this was over,' she said.

V

Antony and Jenny stayed up quite late, but there was no telephone call from Roger.

SUNDAY, 30th MAY

I

He arrived quite early the next morning, however, while they were still at breakfast. Sir Nicholas was with them, having left Moira Pershing the exclusive use of his dining-room. 'I cannot help feeling relieved that Chief Inspector Sykes agreed so readily to take her off our hands,' he was saying when Roger's knock was heard.

Antony went to the door, pretty sure whom he would find there. 'If he gets the early train as he promised he'll be here by noon,' he said over his shoulder as he crossed the room. A moment later he was back again, with Roger at his heels.

If Farrell was at all taken aback by the enlarged audience that awaited him, he didn't show it. He had met Miss Lang-horne before, so there were no introductions to be made. 'I understood from Antony that we might expect to hear from you last night,' said Sir Nicholas, who regarded the Farrells as family and reserved to himself the right of criticising them. 'Does that mean that you have no news for us?'

'On the contrary, Mr. Tremlett was far more helpful than I expected,' said Roger, looking round as though to ensure that he had their full attention. 'That was the trouble, really, he had a lot to tell me, more than was useful; and as he seemed to want to make a night of it, I didn't see how I could refuse. I left him, gently fuddled, at about half-past one, and I thought that was too late to start telephoning.'

'Which of you – ?' enquired Sir Nicholas. Roger grinned at him.

'I have a harder head than that,' he said.

170

'Well, before you put us in the picture there are certain developments to describe to you,' said Sir Nicholas, apparently unconscious that he had thereby very nearly won both Antony's and Jenny's undying hatred. 'Why don't you tell Roger about your visitor yesterday evening, Antony?'

'But –'

'Think he should know,' said Vera unexpectedly. Antony gave her a reproachful look, and resigned himself to the inevitable. The story, however, as he recounted it, was not a long one.

'I wish you would always be as succinct as that in your reports, my dear boy,' said Sir Nicholas cordially, when he had finished.

'But you're still determined to find Mr. X, if you can,' asked Roger, anxious to get the record straight.

'It's just as important today as it was yesterday,' said Antony. The look he gave his friend forbade him to pursue the subject, but Roger wasn't one to require unwieldy explanations.

'Then I'd better tell you the result of my talk with Mr. Tremlett,' he offered. 'I spun him a yarn, didn't know I had such inventive powers –'

'Let me guess,' said Sir Nicholas, who seemed strangely unwilling to hear what Roger had to say. 'You talked about a wager.'

'Something like that. Well, we went all through the financial community, that took some time, as you can imagine; but finally we were left with three names that seemed to fill the bill.'

'Before you tell us, Roger, I think you should know that a suggestion of Miss Langhorne's may have narrowed the field still further. She remembered that Antony had spoken at the time of Mr. X's mentioning a "not proven" verdict. That might mean he's a Scotsman.'

'That's queer,' said Roger, 'one of the names is Scottish.'

'It would be still queerer,' said Maitland solemnly, 'if our

171

quite logical deductions were to have proved wrong. Who is this Scotsman?'

'Ian McGowan. You've heard of McGowan & Company, if you haven't heard of him personally. And, you know, I don't remember ever having seen his picture in the papers.'

Antony was on his feet. 'What we need now is a telephone directory,' he announced, and made for the writing-table, in one of whose drawers he knew he would find what he wanted. 'There are thousands of Mc's,' he grumbled, rustling the pages. 'McGinnis, McGleish, McGonagle . . . here we are! Ian McGowan, 10 Duxberry Place.' He replaced the book, closed the drawer carefully, and when he turned back to the room his face was studiedly expressionless. 'What do you think about that?' he said.

Before replying, Sir Nicholas drained his coffee cup and glanced at his watch. 'It was the wildest of guesses,' he pointed out. 'I cannot help feeling that an unfortunate precedent has been set.' Antony and Jenny exchanged glances, a fact which may or may not have been noticed by Sir Nicholas; in any event, he now turned his attention to Roger. 'It was good of you to take so much trouble in this matter,' he said. 'I am sure Chief Inspector Sykes will be equally grateful.'

It was Antony who answered that. 'Yes, the point is taken, Uncle Nick,' he said.

'I am gratified to hear it.' He came to his feet in his leisurely way as he spoke. 'If we are to be in time for the service it is time we left, Miss Langhorne,' he said then. Vera scrambled to her feet and made for the door.

'With you in a moment,' she promised.

When she had gone Antony looked at his uncle. 'What's all this?' he asked, amused.

'Something you should have thought of yourself, my dear boy, to cater to the tastes of someone who is, after all, your guest, not mine,' said Sir Nicholas, at his blandest. 'We are going to the service at the Greek Orthodox Church in Avery

Street . . . St. George's, I think, but then I tend to think of all Greek Orthodox Churches as St. George's. I am told the singing there is of a very fine order.'

'Who asked her here, I should like to know?' asked Antony in an aggrieved tone, but not until the two church-goers had left. Jenny gave him a look that seemed to pity his ignorance, but before he could demand an explanation she too was making for the door.

'I'll get a cup for you, Roger,' she said, 'and then we may as well be comfortable while we finish our coffee.'

By the time she returned her husband's thoughts had left the subject of his uncle's vagaries. The euphoria with which he had greeted Roger's news had proved only too short-lived. 'It could all be a coincidence,' he said moodily. 'The name, the number of the house, everything.'

'You don't really think that,' said Jenny. Hearing the uneasiness in her voice he gave her a quick smile.

'It's just that I should like to be *sure*,' he explained. 'You know, love, I'm no fonder than the next man of making a fool of myself, and if Sykes is to go bumbling into this man's affairs – '

'Inspector Sykes won't bumble, Antony. You know he's the soul of caution, and can be extremely tactful when he chooses.'

'Well, I'd like to *know*,' he insisted.

'Would you recognise the house if you saw it again?' asked Roger. 'I know you said you were told to walk straight to the door, looking neither to right nor left, but even so – '

'It was a quiet street,' said Maitland, thinking back. 'We left the sound of the traffic behind us when we turned into it. A narrow house, not double-fronted, a room with a bow window at the right of the front door. The door itself, painted black . . . that might have been changed by now. A transom window above the door, shell-shaped, with the number 10 in rather large, gold figures.' He paused, contemplating this catalogue. 'Yes, I think I should recognise it all right.'

'Then you'd better go and see,' said Jenny briskly. She did not look at him as she said this; she was, in fact, stirring her coffee vigorously . . . a quite unnecessary proceeding, as she took neither sugar nor cream.

Antony looked at her for a long moment, weighing up the offer; but the amused understanding of his expression was the only acknowledgment he gave that he recognised the real nobility of the suggestion. 'Where is Duxberry Place anyway?' he demanded.

'Not far from Belgrave Square,' Roger told him. 'If you go down Grosvenor Place . . . we could walk it easily, better than taking the car.'

'Just there and back. There's no reason why we should be more than three-quarters of an hour, Jenny.'

'I'd come with you, only someone's got to be here when Inspector Sykes arrives.' It was obvious from her tone that she would much have preferred the more active role. 'Besides,' she went on, arguing with herself, 'Miss Pershing might get restless. I'd better be here.'

'Thank you love.' To say more than that would be to tear away the pretence she was so valiantly making of feeling no anxiety. Jenny had her own code, and he respected it; just as she respected his. 'Will you come with me, Roger?'

'Of course.'

'You seem to know the way.'

'Uncle Hubert used to live near there,' said Roger. He was trying to catch Jenny's eye, for reassurance, but she was stirring her coffee again. 'I'll go straight home afterwards, Jenny. Meg will be awake by now.'

'Come back to dinner then. I've a feeling,' said Jenny, raising her head and smiling from one of them to the other, 'that a lot of things may have happened by then.'

Later she was to remind them that this time at least she had been a true prophet.

The morning was fine but not too warm, and they walked briskly. Antony was silent and Roger, sensitive to his mood as always, refrained too from speech until he said at last, 'It's the next turning.'

Maitland turned his head then and looked at him rather as though he had forgotten that he was not alone. 'I wonder – ' he said, and did not complete the thought. There was, in any case, no need to do so.

So they turned into Duxberry Place, a narrow street, not very long. The numbering started on the left side at 2, so they walked along the right-hand pavement and counted the houses opposite as they went. But there was really no need to do so, the number 10 in gold figures showed boldly enough on the glass above the black door. 'That's it all right,' he said then in a low voice, almost as though he were afraid of being overheard. 'If Mr. Ian McGowan who lives there now is the same man – '

'That will be for Sykes to find out,' said Roger, taking his arm. 'I don't think there's any doubt about it myself, you can carry coincidence just so far.'

'I suppose you're right,' said Antony. He sighed, as though he still wasn't quite satisfied. 'Let's walk to the end of the street and back, then it won't look as though we came especially to see number 10.'

'All right.' Roger fell into step beside him. 'It may be a good idea, if anyone was watching us. I had the idea – '

'Yes, I saw it too. The curtain moved,' said Antony. 'I wonder if Mr. McGowan's recollections of me are as vivid as mine are of him.'

'He'd remember,' said Roger positively.

'Yes, I dare say. Perhaps we'd better not pass the house

again, Roger. Or is this' – his footsteps slowed as he spoke – 'a dead end?'

'Yes, it is. I'd forgotten. Does it matter?' he added, looking rather curiously at his friend. 'Even if that is the house, even if you were seen and recognised, they can't start anything in the open street.'

'Don't be too sure. He's a resolute man, and he's got a lot to lose.'

'But – '

'Look around you,' Roger looked, and as he did so a little of his self-confidence left him. The street was quiet, too quiet, the sound of traffic came only faintly from the busier street they had left, and there was nobody about; Duxberry Place itself seemed sunk deep in its sabbath torpor. 'We'll go back now,' Antony went on, beginning to retrace his steps, 'but for heaven's sake, Roger – '

Roger was never to know what the advice would have been. They were abreast of number 12 when the door of number 10 opened and two men came out. The first and taller of the two Maitland recognised immediately as the courier who had escorted him to his meeting with Mr. X so many years ago, but that wasn't to say that Kenneth hadn't changed. There was still the rather long, craggy face – another Scotsman, perhaps? – but his frame had filled out. He looked tougher, harder, a man who would stop at nothing; at the same time there was a hint of feverishness about him that Antony noted with a sinking heart. He would only too easily be goaded into action. But perhaps, after all . . .

To the other man he accorded less attention. He was short and stocky and determined-looking. The important thing about both of them – a thing to which Antony hoped Roger was giving due attention – was that each had a hand in the pocket of his jacket. And they stood now, squarely, across the path.

'We meet again, Mr. Maitland,' said Kenneth, rather as if the meeting was something he had been looking forward to for a long time. 'Mr. McGowan would like a word with you.'

For a moment Antony stood quite still. 'There's a coincidence for you, if you like, Roger,' he said then, lightly. And added, in a more urgent tone, 'Don't take any chances with them. They mean business.'

Roger had no intention of taking any chances. At the moment he was still more angry than afraid but he was no actor and he couldn't quite match his companion's lightness of tone. 'I think they might find it inconvenient to shoot us here,' he said, doing his best to make the words a question.

'I don't know who you are, but you're with *him* and that's quite sufficient provocation,' said Kenneth, jerking his head in Maitland's direction. 'But perhaps I should explain that even in this area there is the occasional robbery with violence. No one would hear the shots, I assure you, and if anyone should arrive inconveniently on the scene . . . why, we're playing the good Samaritan, that's all.'

'I see.' Antony glanced warningly in Roger's direction and added, 'We'll come.' Farrell gave a last, incredulous look around him; but you never knew with Antony, he would play the scene his own way, better leave it to him. So he followed his friend, not too unwillingly, through the open door of number 10.

As they went into the hall Maitland was saying to the taller of the two men – the shorter, with Roger, brought up the rear – 'I remember you too, of course. Kenneth, isn't it? I'm sorry to be familiar, but I never knew your full name.'

'And you don't need to know it now,' said Kenneth grimly.

'You had a gun that time too,' said Antony, rather as if he were congratulating the other man on a display of the social graces. 'Kenneth was my escort when I visited this house before,' he added, turning to address his remarks to Roger. 'He favours a small calibre pistol with a silencer, which I imagine is exactly what he has in his pocket now. So you see – '

177

'That's enough,' said Kenneth, exasperated, giving him a shove in the direction of the door on the right of the hall, which also stood open.

Maitland took a moment to regain his balance, said, 'Come on, Roger,' and walked into the room. 'Mr. X, I presume,' he said, almost as blandly as Sir Nicholas himself might have done.

III

Sir Nicholas Harding and Miss Vera Langhorne returned to the house in Kempenfeldt Square shortly after noon. By rights they should both have been in that state of well-being that listening to good music induces, but each was conscious of a mood of sobriety in the other, very far from this. Once inside the house, Vera was making for the staircase when her companion's voice stopped her.

'Come into the study for a moment,' said Sir Nicholas. 'I want a word with you.'

She preceded him into the room, which was his favourite and the one he commonly used. 'You're worried,' she said as she reached the hearth and turned to face him. The words sounded like an accusation.

'I had hoped,' said Sir Nicholas, halting in his turn half-way across the room, 'that the fact was not apparent.'

'Do a pretty good job of hiding it,' Vera admitted.

'I'm glad you think so. The feeling is not quite logical,' he went on, 'because with Miss Pershing's evidence there is no need to worry any longer about Philip Brady; and if Antony has identified Mr. X as Ian McGowan correctly the police can take it from there. Chief Inspector Sykes has always maintained that once you know where to look there is a very good chance of finding what you're looking for.'

'That, at least, sounds logical,' said Vera encouragingly.

'So I don't know why I should be worried, but I am.

Perhaps it is a reflection of Jenny's mood, which would explain matters. She hasn't an ounce of logic in her body.'

'Jenny,' said Vera roundly, 'is a darling.'

Sir Nicholas smiled at her. 'Strictly between the two of us,' he said, 'she is. But that isn't what I brought you here to say to you, my dear Vera.'

'Isn't it?' she asked him. She sounded puzzled.

'I wanted to ask you how you feel now about living in London. It would be a great change,' he pointed out, 'from Chedcombe.'

'Shown me a great deal in the last couple of days,' said Vera, meeting his eye with something of belligerence in her own. 'Trying to tempt me here with the promise of concerts, operas, plays. Wouldn't move for that reason, you know.'

This was too much for Sir Nicholas, perhaps the accusation came too close to the bone. 'Damn it all, woman,' he said explosively, 'I'm asking you to be my wife.'

'Is that what you meant?' For a long moment Vera looked at him, but there was, after all, no trace of guile in her make-up. She smiled then, but without her usual grimness. 'Should like that above all things,' she said.

IV

The room into which they walked (the centre of the spider's web, thought Roger, rather melodramatically) was immediately familiar to Antony. Nothing in the big, book-lined room seemed to have changed, except that he was now seeing it in daylight. And he had never been in any danger of forgetting the man who now stood quietly waiting for them: a slightly-built man, who did not seem to have aged at all since last they met, with fair, thinning hair carefully arranged and an air of quiet elegance. 'I think you know very well who I am, Mr. Maitland,' he said now, in the rather high-pitched voice that was also so well remembered. 'Perhaps you will introduce me to your friend.'

'No need for that,' said Antony quickly.

'As you wish. I made it my business after our last encounter – was it six years ago? – to find out more about you, including the names of your intimate friends. But if you are afraid that after I have dealt with you I shall put myself to the trouble of revenging myself also on your families, you may dismiss the thought from your mind. I do not believe in violence for its own sake.'

'You will admit, however, that your affairs seem to have been attended with a good deal of violence these last few months.' This was said with an amused look; McGowan's eyes met his unsmilingly. They were cold, pale eyes, that also Antony found he remembered very well, and something uncomfortably like a shiver went down his spine now that he met them directly.

'That is not important.' It was obvious that McGowan was not a man who took kindly to criticism. 'You and your friend . . . I presume he is in your confidence.' Maitland did not speak, though the movement of his hand might have been taken as a denial. 'So,' the quiet voice went on, still that of a man dealing rather impatiently with something that should have been beneath his notice, 'you need not trouble to deny it. His being here with you is proof enough for me.'

Antony was aware of Roger, who had come up beside him, breathing deeply as though under the stress of some strong emotion. He could only hope that his friend, a man of action by choice, would for the moment leave matters in his hands. 'Your invitation was rather pressing,' he said, 'but I don't really see what good this talk will do.'

'It will . . . delay your deaths for a little,' said Ian McGowan, smiling for the first time. 'Come now, Mr. Maitland, while there's life there's hope. Aren't you interested in protracting the conversation?'

Roger had evidently been looking about him. He said

now, forcefully, 'Rubbish!' and laid a hand on Antony's arm. 'What's to stop us from leaving?' he asked.

'I should not, of course, endeavour to dissuade you myself,' said the quiet man, 'but you wouldn't get past the door, you know.'

Antony said, 'Don't try it, Roger,' and just for a moment let some of the urgency he felt colour his tone. And then, turning back to McGowan, 'There are things I should like to ask you,' he admitted.

'As you wish. But my question to you must have priority. When Harley died I thought my connection with Northdean was finally severed. How did you track me down?'

'I'm afraid I must say, through your own carelessness,' said Antony. He was choosing his words with some care, and thought the effort was worth it when he saw the quick flush of anger on his adversary's cheeks. 'I was looking for a Scot –'

'I have no accent!'

'No, but one phrase in particular that you used . . . you also said, you know, that you were a good deal more influential than the man in number 10 Downing Street. When I thought about that seriously – and I admit it was only during the last few days – the idea of power led me to money, a reasonable enough equation in today's terms. You have made a pretty exalted position for yourself in the financial world, Mr. McGowan. Wasn't that enough for you? Why did you branch out into crime?'

Strangely, the other man seemed willing to answer the question, taking his time, but speaking readily enough. 'The influence that the head of a great financial house wields is not inconsiderable,' he said, 'but it has its limits. As a master in my chosen profession, unknown to all except a very few of my associates, my power is literally bounded only by my own desires. Isn't there a fascination' – he was warming to his theme as he spoke – 'in flouting the law of the land . . . the absurd law that forbids us to deal with our neighbours in Russia, for example, that forbids us to do what we like with our own wealth? It is –'

'If you're going to give us a lecture on the currency regulations you may spare your pains,' said Antony, interrupting him in full flow. 'You said that you'd answer my questions, or rather you implied that you might. When things began to go wrong in Northdean, how did you arrange matters? Wholesale bribery, or threats?'

'That, Mr. Maitland, was no concern of mine. Knowing Harley I imagine that the – the force of his personality had something to do with it. There were also sums of money disbursed, I did not question his accounting.'

'I see. What had Philip Brady done to you, I wonder, that you should sacrifice him so ruthlesly?'

'Brady? The inquisitive policeman? He was in my way,' said McGowan, as though this should be obvious.

'And when you – how did you put it? – decided to sever your connection with Northdean, Harley was in your way too?'

'He knew who I was,' said McGowan simply. 'And I did not trust you, Mr. Maitland; it seems I was right in that. But I did not expect that you would track me down, or that, having done so, you would be quite so foolhardy as to allow me to know it.'

'That brings us to the next point,' said Antony conversationally. 'Who is your hired assassin at the moment? I don't imagine you killed Harley yourself. As for poor Dobell –'

'Dobell was expendable. Since you are so curious I don't mind telling you that Harley took care of that matter himself. Who killed Harley, in his turn, is no concern of yours.'

'Kenneth, I imagine. Was it Kenneth? He seems to have matured a good deal since I saw him last.' Farrell again made a movement and he added, without looking at him, 'Don't be impatient, Roger. Mr. McGowan is just going to tell us how he proposes to arrange for our demise, and get away with it.'

'I shall do nothing in a hurry.' The man whom for so long he had referred to as Mr. X sounded supremely sure of himself. 'You will find, however, in case you have any doubts on the point,' he added courteously to Roger, 'that my staff is quite large enough and quite capable enough to ensure your safe keeping until I am at leisure to deal with the matter. Tonight, perhaps – '

'If you think – ' began Roger furiously, and was silenced as much by McGowan's considering look as by Antony's gesture.

'I know better than to leave anything to chance,' said McGowan, still with his eyes on Roger's face. 'Mr. Maitland, I know, is a man of some ingenuity, you yourself I should say are of an impetuous nature. But if you are thinking of attacking me and making a dash for the door, let me assure you it would only be to precipate the inevitable.'

Antony, while this exchange had been going on, had moved a little so that now he stood with his back to the window with the doorway well within his range of vision. He was also quite near the desk. He said – and perhaps his casual tone did more to calm Roger than anything else could have done – 'You're proposing to have us tied up and gagged in the meantime, I presume. I should warn you, perhaps, that your – your minions won't find it all that easy.'

'I think there are sufficient of them to manage, Mr. Maitland, particularly when Kenneth's gun is an added persuader. I know of your disability, you see, and though your friend is no doubt a tough man in a brawl – '

'That isn't quite the point.' If the reference to his injured shoulder had angered him, as Roger knew well enough it would have done, he gave no sign. 'As you say, a gun is a gun, and I only wish I had known I was to have the pleasure of this meeting. But that isn't the point either. I was asking you about Kenneth. Don't you think it's time we had him in?' As he spoke his right hand shot out and picked up the heavy glass paper-weight from the desk. This he transferred swiftly to his left hand, and – before his enemy had time to utter a protest – threw it at the door. It landed solidly in the centre, a little above the knob, with a bang lound enough to be startling in the silent house. And almost before it had bounced back onto the carpet the door was flung open and Kenneth appeared, gun in hand, with his shorter companion at his elbow.

'Come in, Kenneth,' said Antony cordially. 'Mr. McGowan has a job of work for you.' He turned to look at his enemy. 'You don't need them both, do you? The chauffeur – it is your chauffeur, isn't it? – can wait outside.'

'You can both go.' McGowan's voice had a coldness that had not been there before. 'I think Mr. Maitland has sufficiently indulged his sense of humour for the time being.'

'But I want Kenneth to stay,' Antony put in quickly. The chauffeur had already disappeared into the hall again. 'Come in and shut the door, won't you?' Maitland added. 'There's something you ought to know. Something I think you will find interesting.'

Kenneth glanced uncertainly at his employer, who looked back at him impassively. Then, eyeing Maitland warily now, he advanced a few paces into the room and closed the door firmly behind him. 'You may need me,' he said, as if to explain his action, but there was no trace of apology in his tone.

Roger was very quiet now, obviously he had decided to let Antony play this his own way; but he had edged round a little so that his back was no longer to the door, and though he was a foot or two from his friend he had an equally good view of the other two men. McGowan made no reply to his subordinate's remark, but Maitland said, 'That's better,' approvingly, and then for the moment fell silent.

He had been right, he was thinking, in forming the opinion that Kenneth had changed with the years. His attitude towards his principal, for instance; it was still respectful, but held now no trace of the subservient. Another thing, as had been obvious from the moment they met in the street, he was as nervous as a cat. Perhaps he didn't like his new role, that of first murderer; perhaps . . . but speculation was useless, the thing was it might give him the chance he wanted, the chance he so badly needed if what had started out as an innocent expedition wasn't to end in disaster. As even now it so easily might.

'In a few minutes,' he said, addressing Kenneth directly, 'you are going to be ordered to take certain steps that will lead, eventually, to our murder. And I think, too, that you are going to be ordered to carry out the killing yourself.'

Without relaxing his vigilance for a moment, Kenneth asked his employer, 'Is that true?'

'Substantially,' McGowan told him. He too was watching Maitland now.

'It makes no odds,' said Kenneth. If his tone was meant to be jaunty it was a dismal failure.

'No, I'm sure. You've graduated to higher things than being a messenger boy, haven't you?' Maitland's tone was casual, almost playful, but Roger was as conscious of his tension as if he had shouted the fact aloud. 'But there are things you ought to know if you are to go ahead and carry out instructions.'

'What things?' Compared with McGowan's rather high-pitched tones, Kenneth's voice was almost a growl.

'Well first, half London knows we're here. If we disappear there'll be questions asked . . . don't you think?'

Kenneth seemed to hesitate, and now he looked uncertainly again at his principal. McGowan said smoothly, 'I don't think you need trouble yourself about that. I have been expecting some such statement ever since these gentlemen joined me. I don't imagine there's a shred of truth in it.'

'Oh, but there is. The people who know we're here include

Chief Inspector Sykes of Scotland Yard. You may have heard of him.'

'Now I know you're lying,' said McGowan triumphantly. 'Sykes is in Northdean.'

'You have a good spy service, but this time they haven't kept you quite up to date. Sykes is on his way here. In fact,' – he glanced at his watch – 'I imagine he's in a taxi at this moment, between Paddington and Kempenfeldt Square.'

'A good story,' said McGowan judiciously. 'But only a story. I know too much about you, Mr. Maitland; you are not used to working on terms of confidentiality with the police. You will disregard it, Kenneth.'

'Not if you're wise.' That was Antony, following hard on a possible advantage. 'You don't see the full beauty of the scheme yet. *You* do the work, *you* get the life sentence for murder, *he* goes free. And I bet he has half his assets safely abroad, so that he could skip the country if things got too hot for him. Isn't that true?' With the last words he turned sharply to face McGowan, and they came like a whiplash. It was a trick Roger had seen him use in court, but now it was only partially successful.

'There's no need for dramatics, Mr. Maitland,' said McGowan easily. 'I've only done what a prudent man would do.'

'That's all very well for you. But did you advise . . . Kenneth, for instance, to take a similar precaution?' That was a shot in the dark, and – miraculously – it came off.

'No, he didn't,' said Kenneth. And suddenly the whole atmosphere in the room was changed. 'I'll not be left here to carry the can,' he added, and there was a certain viciousness in his tone.

'My dear Kenneth, surely you know there's no question of that.' Predictably, McGowan showed no sign of being disturbed. And perhaps to demonstrate his calmness he added reproachfully, 'If you must use slang, at least let it be up to date.' That was greeted by silence, so that he went on more urgently, 'Have I ever failed you? There's no need at all for these recriminations. If you follow my instructions to the letter – '

'That's just the trouble, isn't it?' Maitland had seen the weak line in the chain and meant to see that it got as much strain as possible. 'The demands on you have been growing, haven't they, Kenneth? Not just a matter of taking messages, of acting as a courier as your employer so quaintly put it. When you killed Harley – '

'How did you know that?'

'My dear chap, everyone knows it. I know it, Chief Inspector Sykes knows it. It's only a matter of time – '

'You told me it was fool-proof.' Kenneth's attention wavered as he turned on McGowan angrily. 'You said no one would ever know it wasn't an accident.'

'It seems I was wrong.' (Would the man never show any sign of human weakness?) 'But you really need not worry,' McGowan added. 'To know it was murder is not the same as proving that you were the murderer.'

'Do you want to stand trial?' asked Maitland. Kenneth's agitation was very apparent now. 'Don't you realise that when the police start looking – ' But again he wasn't allowed to finish.

'These two men are the only ones who can link you with the events in Northdean. When they are dead – '

'When I've killed them, you mean.'

'Yes, I do mean that.' (It wasn't going to do any good; McGowan was staring his younger accomplice down.)

Antony said, without much hope, 'He's been using you, Kenneth, all along the line. And now that it's come to murder – ' And suddenly Kenneth broke.

'Well, I'm through doing your dirty work for you.' He was babbling, almost incoherent. 'To go to prison and think of you, living it up abroad.'

'There is no question of that. No one can prove anything against me . . . except these two men. But I should remind you that the police might be interested in some of your activities, Kenneth. You would be wiser to obey me.'

Those were the last words he spoke. Kenneth, with a sudden appearance of calm that must have been illusory, took careful aim and shot him through the head.

And at the same moment, Roger sprang, dragged down the assassin's gun hand so that the second shot went harmlessly into the carpet, and then twisted Kenneth's arm until the gun, too, dropped to the floor. Antony picked it up, and after a moment Kenneth stopped struggling and stood quite quietly, looking from one to the other of them. 'I looked up to him for years,' he said, 'admired him, did everything he asked of me. Even when . . . but murder's different. I hadn't reckoned on that.'

'Then why – ?' said Roger, rather breathlessly. But Kenneth was silent again, and Antony answered for him.

'Perhaps it comes easier the second time,' he said, and handed the gun to his friend. 'You'd better take this thing, and remember the chauffeur may have heard the shot, even though it was silenced. If he did, he'll be in at a run and you'll have to keep an eye on both of them.'

'Understood,' said Roger.

'There isn't anything to be done for McGowan,' said Antony a moment later. He walked across the room to where the telephone stood on a low table. 'I think this is where we talk to Sykes,' he went on, picking up the receiver and preparing to dial his own number. 'If he's arrived, that is.'

Jenny got the message just as the Chief Inspector, preceded by Miss Langhorne and followed by Sir Nicholas, walked through the living-room door. She said afterwards that she hadn't even had time to grow anxious; Antony made no comment on that, but knew better than to believe her.

V

It was late afternoon before the interviews with the police were finished, and after that there was Sir Nicholas to face. Maitland was frankly expecting ructions; not only had he deliberately – as his uncle was sure to assert – involved himself in a dangerous situation, but Ian McGowan was well known to the gentlemen of the press and his death was bound to cause an uproar. It was surprising, therefore, to find Uncle Nick in an apparently mellow frame of mind, with nothing more to say than 'All's well that ends well.' When Antony, rather alarmed by this mood of forbearance, pointed out himself the certainty that the newspapers were about to have a field day the older man did say, dryly, 'It won't be the first time.' But really nobody could cavil at that. Antony went upstairs to join Jenny and Vera extremely puzzled and still a little worried.

Roger had gone straight home, but returned in time for dinner bringing Meg with him. Sir Nicholas had arrived just before them, bringing three bottles of champagne, and repaired directly to the kitchen to supervise the putting of them on ice. When he returned to the living-room with Jenny it was to hear Meg saying plaintively, 'I can't make head or tail of this story Roger's been telling me. If this Mr. McGowan and Kenneth were partners, why did Kenneth shoot him?'

'He was sulky at first but he did talk to Sykes eventually,' Antony told her. He was pouring sherry, and seemed more concerned with that simple task than with Meg's question. 'He admired McGowan for being successful, and didn't really mind at all that some of the jobs he was required to do had a criminal flavour. But he did jib at murder, and only consented to kill Harley because his employer put some pressure on him . . . blackmailing him with his own past misdeeds, in other words.'

'I don't see why Kenneth fell for that,' said Jenny. She had again her serene look, to her husband's contentment, but she knew well enough that he was still on edge.

'You must remember McGowan's position, his apparently impregnable position,' Antony told her. 'He persuaded Kenneth that the police would believe that he had known nothing of what was going on. That rankled, it must have rankled a great deal, so that when I started trying to put a wedge between them Kenneth just lost his head.'

'Yes, that was really clever of you, darling,' said Meg. 'So much neater than a trial.'

Antony passed the last of the sherry, and took his own glass to place on the mantelpiece. 'I didn't know it was going to lead to another murder,' he protested. 'It just seemed a good idea on general principles.'

'And may I remind you that there will be a trial . . . Kenneth's,' Sir Nicholas put in. Antony glanced at him, expecting that this was the prelude to some more acid comment, but the genial mood still seemed to persist. His uncle returned his look with a bland one. 'I also have to report,' he went on, 'that Miss Pershing is no longer in possession of my spare room. It was thoughtful of you, Antony, to remind Chief Inspector Sykes to send someone to fetch her. That was a responsibility I did not altogether relish.'

'She's made a statement to the police, so that's all right,' said Antony, and for the first time his tone was altogether one of satisfaction. 'And I had a long conversation on the telephone with Peter Gibson, so he's quite happy, even though Brady can't possibly be released for a day or two. In fact,' – he looked at Jenny, who met his eyes with her customary unruffled air – 'an eminently satisfactory conclusion all round. Though I still think, Uncle Nick, it's a gruesome idea to celebrate Mr. X's demise with champagne.'

'You would indeed be right if that was what I intended,'

said Sir Nicholas with mock seriousness. If he had lost his eloquence earlier in the day, it had now returned to him in full measure. 'The champagne is certainly a celebration, but for quite another cause.' He looked around him, making sure that he had their full attention. Vera spilled her sherry, but no-one took any notice of that. Jenny began to laugh. 'I have to tell you' – nothing could have exceeded the solemnity of the announcement – 'that Miss Vera Langhorne has done me the honour of accepting my proposal of marriage. And I have also to tell you,' – his eyes were on Vera now and Antony (pleased, incredulous) could no longer be in any doubt that his uncle was deeply moved – 'I have to tell you,' said Sir Nicholas earnestly, 'that she wouldn't think of leaving Chedcombe just for the concerts.'